SHERLOCK HOLMES
AND MR. MAC

'Mr. Mac', as Sherlock Holmes calls him, is the talented young Inspector Alec MacDonald. Though he's out to make his mark at Scotland Yard, some baffling new cases have him seeking assistance from the great detective; and the two, along with the stalwart Doctor Watson, join forces. In *The Affair of Lady Westcott's Lost Ruby*, the seemingly mundane disappearance of an elderly lady's pet leads to unexpectedly sinister consequences, while in *The Unseen Assassin*, a mysterious marksman embarks upon a serial killing spree across London.

Books by Gary Lovisi
in the Linford Mystery Library:

SHERLOCK HOLMES AND
THE CROSBY MURDERS

THE SECRET FILES OF
SHERLOCK HOLMES

MURDER OF A BOOKSELLER

THE PLOT AGAINST
SHERLOCK HOLMES

GARY LOVISI

SHERLOCK HOLMES AND MR. MAC

Complete and Unabridged

LINFORD
Leicester

First published in Great Britain

First Linford Edition
published 2017

*A catalogue record for this book is available
from the British Library.*

ISBN 978–1–4448–3456–7

Published by
F. A. Thorpe (Publishing)
Anstey, Leicestershire

Set by Words & Graphics Ltd.
Anstey, Leicestershire
Printed and bound in Great Britain by
T. J. International Ltd., Padstow, Cornwall

This book is printed on acid-free paper

The Affair of
Lady Westcott's
Lost Ruby

1

221B Baker Street

'I have often noticed that crime can become a double-edged sword, Watson,' Sherlock Holmes mentioned to me one brisk autumn day in 1890.

'How so?' I prompted him eagerly.

Holmes smiled rather enigmatically. 'The law of unintended consequences, of course. All actions precipitate reactions — some of which cannot be anticipated and may make matters worse, from our point of view, in solving criminal cases. And of course, usually from the point of view of the criminal as well, often landing them in prison. You are trying to bait me, eh, my friend?'

Holmes was in one of his rare talkative moods, and I decided to take advantage of it to press him to recount one of his hitherto unrecorded cases. Who knew what gem I might unearth?

'Or perhaps it is you who are trying to whet my appetite to hear a new story? Are you referring to a specific case?' I was baiting him now!

'Hah!' Holmes laughed. 'You seem eager enough!'

'Of course! I am always ready. I would certainly like to hear whatever you have to say, upon whatever topic, but especially if you feel like talking about one of the cases I have yet to record.'

'Well, you are in luck, old man. I am certainly in the mood for talk now. So ask away!'

I paused. Well, that put me in a quandary. I was actually taken aback by his seemingly open-ended invitation to ask him whatever I would ask him, upon any topic I chose. It was like opening Pandora's Box. A million questions crossed my mind, each one fighting for dominance. I hardly even knew what to ask him. I was suddenly silent, thinking.

Holmes smiled faintly. 'Perhaps I should begin?'

'Perhaps you should. Yes, please do,' I replied, a bit perplexed by this sudden turn of events. I had known this man for many years, and I can tell you that it was most unusual for Holmes to be as open and forthcoming as he appeared to be now. Did I sense an ulterior motive?

There was a long pause, Holmes obviously considering his words carefully, while I was taking deep breaths of nervous eager anticipation.

Sherlock Holmes began by stating briskly, 'Well, Watson, I have first to tell you that I have lately read your chronicle of my Brilstone Manor Case — what you have so melodramatically entitled 'The Valley of Fear'.'

'Yes, I am always interested to hear your comments on what I have written up of your cases.'

He gave me a rather dour frown. 'Ah-hem! Really, old man, you must be more specific and pander less to popular taste. Your choice of title makes the case sound like some cheap and lurid penny dreadful. I do not think that you should offer this one for publication at this time. Certainly not for some years, at any rate. That is my decision for the present, and I must ask you to accept that prohibition.'

I said not a word, but I was surely crestfallen by these words.

'Oh, cheer up, old man. In the writing of it, I find it to be a quite adequate narrative, if a rather tall tale, as usual.'

'Holmes, I feel you are too hard on me in this regard. You must make some allowances for poetic license and the popular taste.'

'Hah! Never!' My companion chortled in a derisive tone.

'Holmes!'

'Oh, very well; in truth it is not at all bad. The Pennsylvania part concerning Birdy Edwards and the Scowrers was fine — rather well done, actually. But please do not publish it until I give you my permission to do so. I would not have this one out there so soon.'

'Of course.' I nodded my acknowledgement with these two grudging words at his stern prohibition, which I would of course respect, though I was severely disappointed. Then I dared ask him, 'And what of the preamble concerning the affair at Brilstone Manor House?'

'Hmm . . . well, yes, I suppose you had all the facts in order there as well,' Holmes admitted, but with some obvious reluctance. He was not a man overly fond of giving praise unless it was for some striking accomplishment, and only if well deserved.

I sat there wearing my stoic face, nevertheless glowing inside due to his praise, however faintly delivered. Then I ventured, 'Inspector Alec MacDonald acquitted himself very well in that case, did he not?'

'He surely did, Watson. I expected great things from that young Scot and he has not disappointed.'

I thought about the man and the words I had written about him in the story that Holmes had now prohibited me from publishing:

Those were the early days at the end of the '80s, when Alec MacDonald was far from having attained the national fame which he has now achieved. He was a young and trusted member of the detective force, who had distinguished himself in several cases which had been entrusted to him. His tall, bony figure gave promise of exceptional physical strength, while his great cranium and deep-set, lustrous eyes spoke no less clearly of the keen intelligence that twinkled out from behind his bushy eyebrows. He was a silent, precise man with a dour nature and a hard Aberdonian accent.

Twice already in his career had Holmes helped him to attain success, his own sole reward being the intellectual joy of the problem. For this reason the affection and respect of the Scotsman for his amateur colleague were profound, and he showed them by the frankness with which he consulted Holmes in every difficulty. Mediocrity knows nothing higher than itself, but talent instantly recognizes genius, and MacDonald had talent enough for his profession to enable him to perceive that there was no humiliation in seeking the assistance of one who had already stood alone in Europe, both in his gifts and in his experience. Holmes *was not prone to friendship, but he was tolerant of the big Scotsman, and smiled at the sight of him.*

'I wonder how he is getting along,' I mused.

'Oh, I am sure he is making a name for himself at the Yard,' Holmes added rather off-handedly, apparently a bit piqued by my bringing up the subject of Inspector MacDonald. The inspector had not come to Holmes with a case for some time now. Was he purposely staying away? I wondered. My companion's manner had suddenly changed now also. Holmes was like that: mercurial in temperament as well as thought. I feared that the mood of talkativeness that had come upon him so suddenly just moments before had now left him completely.

'What is it, Holmes?'

'Just thinking, old man; rearranging the furniture in the attic of my mind.'

I shrugged. Holmes often spoke in such enigmatic terms. I put down my pipe, then stood up and walked towards the window of our sitting room. I opened it to allow in some of the brisk autumn breeze to air out our stuffy smoke-filled rooms. Perhaps the sharp, cool air would improve my friend's mood or catch his attention.

As I opened the window, I casually looked down upon Baker Street to view with approval that the small world around us appeared as orderly and organized as always. I noted a group of young boys upon a stoop across the street, Wiggins and some of the young fellows he ran with that Holmes sometimes made use of in cases. Then nearby on the street below I was surprised to spot a familiar figure that I recognized immediately. I instantly blurted out, 'It is him, Holmes!'

'Him?' my companion repeated in a languid tone, not moving a muscle, though I noticed his eyebrows were raised in evident curiosity.

'He is walking along Baker Street right this minute.'

'Do you mean Mr. Mac?' Holmes replied with a further hint of curiosity.

'Yes, I do.'

'Well do tell!'

'Yes, it is certainly him. Who could ever fail to recognize the man? He is a most singular person in form and dress. Tall and slim, not unlike yourself. I wonder what he is up to.'

'So do I.'

'Well, he is walking rather briskly down Baker Street right now,' I stated, watching him eagerly. 'Maybe he's coming here.'

'He's not coming here,' Holmes stated as he looked over at the window with repressed curiosity. I could tell he was trying to hold back a growing impatient excitement. I knew my companion held considerable respect for Mr. Mac, as he was fond of calling the large dour Scot, and he knew that when the man came to him with a case, it would be a real challenge. And Sherlock Holmes always loved a challenge!

I watched the man's steps carefully. MacDonald was now directly across from 221, but then instead of crossing the street to our door, he continued on down the street and was soon gone from my view. I told my friend, 'No, it does not appear he is coming here at all.'

Holmes steepled his fingers in thoughtful contemplation, then nodded. 'However, he certainly will when he is ready for us. The double-edged sword I spoke of earlier, my friend. Mr. Mac is a man in rapid motion and upon a mission. Who knows where the threads will lead him.'

'Perhaps here, to Baker Street,' I ventured.

'We shall see, but threads can become awfully twisted and complicated.'

I looked over at Holmes, wondering what he meant by that statement. Then I once again looked down below at Baker Street to see if I could get another glimpse of Inspector MacDonald; but he was gone from my sight as if London itself had swallowed him up. Nevertheless, I wondered about the Scotland Yard inspector and what case he might be working on now, and I am sure Sherlock Holmes was thinking the exact same thing.

2

Inspector Alec MacDonald

He was keenly aware of what they were saying about him. He had excellent hearing among his many other keen attributes. He was a Scotland Yard detective, after all; a man who had achieved some notoriety in a highly publicized case last year.

'That's 'im, lads!' The street Arabs who were gathered on a building stoop along Baker Street whispered furtively to each other as he walked briskly by them.

'Aye, they's that matter, like our Mr. Holmes calls this one Mr. Mac. Why, look at him! Ain't he the dapper bloke!'

The man the boys were watching allowed a slim smile to escape his lips. He was certainly well dressed. He wore a starched white shirt with rounded collars and a knotted necktie — all the rage as the newest in men's fashion just then

13

— which gave him a serious formal look that was almost funereal. He was a serious man, and one you did not want to find yourself on the wrong side of.

Scotland Yard Inspector Alec Mac-Donald smiled as he walked by the group of young boys, who continued to whisper in awe about him. He knew them as an unofficial street gang that his friend, Mr. Sherlock Holmes, called his Baker Street Irregulars; and they had proven their use on a number of criminal cases. They were good boys in his book.

MacDonald had known Sherlock Holmes for the last couple of years. The consulting detective had aided him on two earlier cases, and then there had been the big one: the Brilstone Manor murder mystery involving John Douglas and his wife a year back that the two detectives — he official and other consulting — had been deeply involved in. With the new location of Scotland Yard on the Victoria Embankment overlooking the majestic River Thames since 1890, MacDonald and the members of the Metropolitan Police had a new home and a new mission: professional policing.

MacDonald allowed a grim smile that slowly twisted the drooping ends of his long handle-bar mustache as he remembered Sherlock Holmes. Holmes and he had got along rather well. The Great Detective, as MacDonald thought of Holmes fondly, was a most fascinating man, and MacDonald treasured and respected his genius. In return, Holmes respected MacDonald's talent.

The Scotland Yard man thoughtfully remembered the praise Holmes had given him for a case that had been the making of his career at the time. He was a crack detective for sure, and one of the Yard's best prospects. He would have liked to have been involved in the Ripper case back in '88, but his superiors had kept him out of it. That was just the way it was at the Yard sometimes, with the big cases going to the most senior or favored men with influence. Lestrade was one of those highly placed men. It was difficult these days to catch the big cases with so many political power-plays going on. The Ripper case had been a sensation in the newspapers back then, and had never been solved. MacDonald would have loved to have sunk his teeth into that one; for when he was on a case, he was like a starving dog with a meaty bone, and he would never let go until the case was solved, one way or the other. But alas, now he had to focus on the task at hand.

MacDonald continued walking down Baker Street, passing across from Number 221. Holmes had told him once that he was a very talented but practical detective. He now wondered if he was a bit too practical, a bit too sensible, and too regular in his approach to crime. Holmes could be so mercurial, while MacDonald was more by-the-book and tried-and-true in his investigation techniques. The men had different ways of doing things, but their methods were similar and often complementary to one another.

Holmes obviously approved of Mac-Donald; but though he was a young and trusted member of Scotland Yard's detective force, he had yet to really make his mark as a star of the department. He hoped that the opportunity afforded to him by this new investigation would yield that source of satisfaction in his chosen calling he so desperately craved. A new case was always cause for excitement.

This new investigation that Chief Inspector Sir Charles Maine had tasked MacDonald with today seemed promising. It was near the end of a busy day, so he figured to stop by the residence of the victim on his walk home. The case seemed to concern a minor member of the nobility or some such person of the upper class — wealthy to be certain; but much more importantly, there was a missing ruby. There could be promise in solving such a case, and he hastened his footsteps until he reached number 20 on Abercrombie Road.

MacDonald saw that the house was a large three-story brick fortress: a mansion to be sure; a building that oozed wealth and power, privilege and position. He trod up the six steps to the elegant white mahogany front door and briskly struck the shiny large brass knocker. The din his action caused rumbled resoundingly inside and outside the house. It brought to his mind the cacophony caused by a large Oriental temple gong he recalled from his early days as a constable in the Chinese quarter of the city.

After a moment the door was opened, and an older and rather distinguished gentleman in butler livery looked upon him with a world-weary and inquiring gaze.

'I am Inspector Alec MacDonald of Scotland Yard,' he said simply to the man who had answered the door, his thick Aberdeen accent sounding most un-English here in the central environs of London. 'I am here to see your mistress, Mrs. Westcott.'

'Lady Westcott!' the butler corrected firmly.

'All right,' MacDonald allowed. He was not one to be overly impressed with titles, but if this case involved a member of the nobility he was willing to play along. 'Yes, Lady Westcott.'

'Then you are here to see my lady about her lost ruby?'

'Yes.'

'Please follow me.'

The butler led MacDonald into the large foyer and then up an elaborate circular staircase. Along the walls the inspector marveled at the many exquisite paintings of what were apparently famous ancestors, some of whom MacDonald thought he could recognize as well-known figures out of British history.

'My mistress is indisposed at the moment, unfortunately, so she will see you from her bedside,' the butler explained, leading his visitor down the hallway to a large closed door at the head of the upper hall.

'I take it she is greatly upset?'

'Very much so, sir,' the butler stated. He seemed a most proper British gentleman's gentleman — or in this case a gentle lady's gentleman.

'Well, I will not detain her any longer than is absolutely necessary for me to gather all the facts I need.'

'Thank you, sir,' the butler stated in obvious relief. 'My mistress is most alarmed and distressed by this sudden loss.'

'I can well understand it,' MacDonald replied with a sharp nod of his head. This certainly appeared to be something of considerable importance. A lost ruby? He wondered how valuable the bauble might be. A hundred thousand pounds? Perhaps a million pounds? There was no telling with such things, and he certainly was no expert in fine gems. However, he would find out. This could just be the one case that might make him, he thought with a dash of excitement in his steps as he followed the butler to the door to the old woman's bedchamber.

Once outside the room, the butler opened the door and escorted Mac-Donald into a sumptuous lady's boudoir; and there, lying upon her back and braced up against a mound of frilly pillows in a large canopied bed, was an aged gentlewoman who appeared quite worried. She looked at MacDonald, noting his presence, but spoke not a word. For a moment he wondered just why she was silent. Had she lost her voice? She was obviously in severe distress. Then the inspector allowed a dour smile, realizing that there could never be any personal conversation in the bedchambers of a lady until he and she had been properly introduced.

'Madam, this is Inspector MacDonald from Scotland Yard,' the butler began. Then he looked upon the policeman. 'Sir, may I present to you my mistress, Lady Anne Westcott.'

'Thank you, Gerald,' the old woman now spoke up, addressing the butler in a tone that indicated he was now dismissed.

The butler offered the most minimal of nods as he left the room, closing the door softly behind him.

Inspector MacDonald cleared his throat at the amusing idea of being alone with Lady Westcott in the privacy of her boudoir.

'Please excuse the irregularity of this interview, Inspector. I am heartbroken and utterly distraught by what has happened. I just want to have my precious ruby returned to me as soon as possible,' she said, obviously holding back tears.

'Of course, madam,' MacDonald stated in an understanding tone and with a nod of his head, but he was eager to get to the facts.

Lady Westcott offered her visitor a chair

across from her bed, but MacDonald immediately declined it. He did not want to become comfortable here; he needed to get to work right away on this case. He quickly took out his pad and pencil, ready to take notes on the questions he was even now forming in his mind.

'Well, Lady Westcott,' MacDonald began, tamping down his accent, 'I am going to ask you some questions now. Please be as detailed as possible in your answers, as something that may seem insignificant to you might offer me some clue that could solve this case.'

'Of course, Inspector.' Lady Westcott gave a flutter of a smile, a ray of hope perhaps now having entered her features as she tried to compose herself and collect her thoughts.

'Now, then,' MacDonald asked, 'how long has your ruby been missing?'

'Since the day before last, Inspector,' she replied, obviously trying to hold back her tears.

The inspector smiled inwardly; these rich old birds were all alike, bound to their money and wealth in their advanced age as if with stout linked chains. Someone should tell them they could not take it with them.

'Now, ma'am . . . '

'I want my precious ruby back!'

MacDonald nodded. 'Of course you do. Now tell me, where was the ruby the last time it was seen by you? And who in your house had access to it?'

Lady Westcott looked at the man sitting across from her blankly, then grew stern, perhaps even angry. 'Inspector, I assure you, this is not a frivolous situation! It is a most serious matter. Please do not anger me!'

MacDonald found himself gobsmacked by her sudden words and tone. What had he said that had seemingly insulted the woman? 'Of course I am serious,' he replied firmly, his Scots accent a bit thick now, wondering exactly what she meant by her words, and what he had said to set her off.

'That is good to hear. My precious ruby is missing,' she stated sternly now, 'and I want her back!'

'Her?' MacDonald echoed, very much

confused now. Then he did a double-take when he realized what exactly he had just heard. He put down his pad and pencil and looked closely at Lady Westcott, lying so disconsolate there in her bed. This was no joke; she appeared to be in complete earnest. He slowly rubbed his chin, mentally counting to ten to control his patience before he spoke. Mr. Holmes had once told him that patience in interviewing witnesses was often crucial to their cooperation. He repeated his short question of a moment before. 'Her?'

'Yes, of course,' Lady Westcott replied in a matter-of-fact tone as if it were the most natural thing in the world.

Inspector MacDonald nodded, marshaled his thoughts and tamped down his growing temper. 'Lady Westcott, can you tell me what, or who, Ruby might be?'

'Why, Ruby is my beloved dog, Inspector. A delightful and perfectly behaved little Yorkshire Terrier.'

Inspector MacDonald, taking in this news and considering the circumstances, suddenly broke into uncontrolled laughter. This must be some kind of joke. He had been had! Royally! Wait until the boys at the Yard heard about this one.

'Nicely done,' he said somewhat sarcastically, still unable to hold back his chagrin. The anger would come later, he knew, but right now he could only laugh because it was such a perfect cock-up that even he saw the outrageous humor in it.

Lady Westcott, however, did not. 'I do not know what you find so amusing, sir. My poor Ruby is out there all alone, somewhere only God knows, cold and hungry for two whole days! She has never run off before; this action is most unusual and quite unlike her. I miss her terribly. I demand satisfaction, Inspector. If my late husband Simon were still with us, I assure you he would wipe that silly smile off your face!'

MacDonald ceased his laughter immediately. He had to take care here. This was no shopkeeper's wife; she was a noblewoman with obvious connections that ran up to Sir Charles himself. If handled improperly, the situation could become a disaster. He also had no wish to offend the old woman. Even though he had been done quite nicely by her, still and all, he realized that he felt sorry for her. She was elderly, seemingly ill, and alone, and not a bit unlike his own beloved mum back in Aberdeen — God bless her! He could see the woman was seriously worried about her poor missing pet. Even so, he was a detective with Scotland Yard — his job was to investigate crimes of robbery and murder, not to find and collect recalcitrant pets.

He grew dour. He could play it tough as well, so he informed her sternly, 'Calling the police under false pretenses, Lady Westcott, can be cause for fines or even prosecution under the law.'

She did not reply, and he instantly felt ashamed he had been so hard on her. He immediately put aside the stinging slight he had felt from the situation, and resolved to deal with the jibes he knew would come from his fellow detectives soon enough when they arose. He did not care. He only felt sorry for the old lady now.

MacDonald looked down at the elderly woman lying there in her bed, sad, imploring him with her eyes and he said softly, 'I apologize for my harsh tone.'

'You should!' Then Lady Westcott began to cry. 'Ruby was my sole companion in this cold lonely world, Inspector. Please, will you find her?'

MacDonald put his pad and pencil away. He went over to the old woman and softly patted her shoulders reassuringly. 'I am sorry about your missing dog, Lady Westcott, but this is hardly a job for the official police. Even if I wanted to help you, my superiors would never allow it. I do not think that I can offer any help in this matter.'

'Go then . . . Get out of my house! You are no help,' she cried, showing her imperious side at being denied the aid she felt she was due.

MacDonald stood his ground. He felt terrible, like a right proper heel, and he was not used to the feeling at all. He did not like it. He wished he could do something to help the old lady, but what could he do?

'Lady Westcott, I am sure that Ruby will turn up before long. Have hope and try to collect yourself.'

'But she is all alone and hungry! I am sure of it!'

'Then perhaps because she is hungry she will come back to the good home that I know she has here with you.'

'You think so?' She brightened a bit.

'Why not?' he asked, flashing her a comforting smile.

The old woman stopped crying and calmed down a bit at his reassuring words. He saw their effect on her and decided to continue with that tack. 'Tell me this — where would Ruby find a better home, or anyone who loved her more than you, Lady Westcott?' he offered with a warm smile.

The elderly woman nodded assuredly at that, and a tiny smile struggled to break through her lips. 'I hope you are right, Inspector. You are a good man, after all.'

MacDonald was touched by her words. 'Be patient, ma'am. I am sure she will return home soon.'

'Thank you.' She sniffled, holding back another barrage of tears.

MacDonald prepared to leave. It was

late and he wanted to get home at the end of a long day, but something here was bothering him. He knew he had to find some way to help this lady.

'I will ring for Gerald to show you out, Inspector,' the old woman said, a bit more calm now. 'And Inspector, thank you for humoring a silly old lady.'

'Think nothing of it,' MacDonald replied, his dour Scot armor now softened to jelly by her words. Then the butler arrived and showed him out of the room and escorted him to the front door.

Before he left the house, MacDonald asked the butler, 'Do you or any of the household staff have any idea what could have happened to the dog?'

'No, sir. Lady Westcott is severely distressed; she dearly loves that animal. It is not like Ruby at all to run off, and no one has seen her since yesterday morning.'

'Where was she last seen, and what was she doing?'

'Running in the back yard along the fence. Lady Westcott allows her the run of the yard. She was barking at something, as usual. She is a small dog, but makes quite a bit of noise, as the smaller breeds often do.'

'Well, then, if you hear anything, will you let me know?'

'Of course, sir,' Gerald said, softening his demeanor a bit. 'And thank you.'

MacDonald nodded. 'Well, here is my card with my address at home and at the Yard.'

'That is most appreciated, sir,' Gerald said, taking the card. Without even looking at it, he deftly placed it in his vest pocket. 'Lady Westcott will be pleased.'

3

Ruby

Inspector Alec MacDonald left the West-cott residence and began the long walk back to his room in Marylebone. He decided not to take a trap or cab, as he had some things on his mind and he wanted to think them through as he walked. The simple matter was that there was something about this Westcott situation that bothered him. It had to do with his feelings about the sad old woman, even though he knew his tough-cop image might suffer if he took this case on. Was he getting soft? Emotional? He realized that he really did not care what others might say; all he wanted to do was to help this woman by finding her lost dog. The old gal was alone and lonely, all by herself, but with a household full of servants. He smiled at that; he also smiled because he knew he would get hell from the fellows at the Yard first thing

31

tomorrow morning once they found out about this. However, as a tried and true copper, there was something else nagging him about this; something he could not put his finger on yet, but which was compelling him to become involved.

He went home to his flat and made a passable dinner, finishing it off with two pints of bitter. He read some of the news stories in the *Times;* the usual murders and scandal on the front pages among the higher classes, with more sinister and brutal crimes committed by the lower classes and foreigners written about in the back pages. Not much out of the ordinary there, so he began to get weary and decided to make it an early night. He prepared for bed, laying down, dog tired, but unable to sleep.

What was it that was bothering him? This damnable Ruby case! That troublesome little dog gone missing just didn't make sense. MacDonald thought about it, and after a while without any success he drifted off to sleep.

He awoke an hour later with a start. He thought of his mentor, Sherlock Holmes.

Now what would the great man do about such a situation? Perhaps nothing. After all, lost dogs were not within Holmes's purview, however unusual the cases were — and this could be unusual. Or so it seemed. Surely Holmes would not view the problem merely as it appeared on the surface; he never assumed anything and took nothing for granted. Surely he would follow the case and see where it led. But just where did it lead?

'Holmes is right: I am too practical; too logical. I need to look between the cracks, under the carpet, behind the motives; then there just may be more to this than some dotty old dowager and her little missing mutt.'

MacDonald rubbed his face and twisted the long ends of his bushy mustache. He knew what he had to do now, and the realization enabled him to soon get back to a dreamless slumber.

★ ★ ★

First thing the next morning, MacDonald went to the Yard and told his superior, Sir

Charles Maine, what had come about from his visit to Lady Westcott.

After Sir Charles finally ceased his laughter about the little dog being missing, he offered the young detective a playful grin. 'Sorry about that, Mac-Donald, but we couldn't ignore the request from the old biddy.'

'I know, sir; I hear she is nobility, or some such thing. She has some influence.'

'Influence, I'll say! But not nobility, my man. She is royalty, somehow related to old Queen Vic herself, though I don't know just how. The details seem rather vague. Anyway, we could not just ignore her request to send someone, and you won. The luck of the draw, old man.'

'I see.'

'Oh, buck up, lad. It's not the end of your career,' Sir Charles said with a smile as he patted his young inspector on the back.

'I've been made a laughing stock, that's all.'

'Sorry, lad, but I had to send someone.'

Alec MacDonald nodded his head in resignation; then he looked full into the face of his superior and asked, 'So why not let me work the case then?'

'Are you serious? It's a lost dog!'

'The old lady really is kind of sweet, and she's very keen on that dog. My work load is light now, so maybe I could spend some time on this between other things?'

Sir Charles Maine shook his head. 'There's too much to do right now.'

'Not enough to have me stop off there yesterday, officially. Now when the rest of the men find out about this, I will be the butt of jokes for a fortnight at least. Why not allow me to see this through?'

'There's nothing *to* see through.'

'There may just be.'

'You think so?' Sir Charles Maine looked carefully at his young inspector. He respected MacDonald, knew the lad had a nose for crime, but he did not like his overtly aggressive attitude. However, he realized the lad might be right; and moreover, politically it might be a good decision to have him placate the old biddy.

'Well?' MacDonald urged.

'On your own time, then.'

'All right.' MacDonald gave Sir Charles a dour grin as he left the chief inspector's office.

* * *

It was the usual mayhem for the Metropolitan Police that day in London. Crimes among the teeming populace in the center of the vast British empire seemed to be almost a national sport in certain precincts of the city these days. There had been a rather ghastly murder in Boxley; then a standard pub fight with the killer picked up by the peelers and injuring two of their best boys. There had been a bloody household stabbing in Wessex, a crime of passion, so-called in the French fashion — it seemed a husband came home a bit too early from the shop to discover his wife canoodling with the butcher from down the street. The butcher and the wife would not be doing that anymore. The husband was found beside the body of his dead wife, crying, and looking at the bloody knife in his hand like it was some mystical artifact of a long-lost civilization. He just kept mumbling, 'The knife would not stop stabbing them!'

MacDonald had seen and heard it all before. The next case of the day was a robbery gone wrong at a hostelry in Limehouse — a nefarious place with the odor of an opium den about it but without any evidence of same. The robber was a lone man with a gun who took off with 50 pounds — quite a haul. The man was recognized as an unemployed factory worker named Stanislaw Porcoro. He was found and arrested. With that bit of work over, the day was done, and MacDonald decided to stop off at the Westcott mansion to see how the old girl was doing.

As he turned the corner at Abercrombie, MacDonald immediately noticed the ominous shrouds of black bunting around the front door as he approached the woman's house. The dour Scotsman was overcome by a feeling of dread. Had the old woman passed away in his absence as a result of the loss of her beloved pet? Or worse — his grim nature was asserting itself now — had she given in to despair and taken her own life? MacDonald knew that distressed people could do some strange things when they felt helpless or hopeless, or that events were swirling out of their control.

With trepidation, MacDonald struck the brass knocker on the front door and waited until it was finally opened by the butler, Gerald. The man looked hard pressed but relieved to see the detective. 'It is good that you have come, Inspector,' he said quietly.

'Lady Westcott?' MacDonald blurted anxiously.

'She is still bed-ridden I am afraid, but . . . You see, the tragic news, I fear, may have unhinged her.'

'What tragic news? I don't understand. When I saw the black bunting on the house, I naturally assumed . . . ' He looked closely at the butler with curious intent. 'Do you mean Ruby?'

'Yes, sir. She was found by the grounds-keeper late last evening. The decaying body had begun to give off a most unpleasant odor.'

MacDonald nodded. 'So what happened?'

Gerald led the inspector into the house and the two talked in whispers in the grand foyer.

'So the dog was found, and it is dead?'

'Not just dead. I am afraid someone killed it intentionally.'

'How so?' MacDonald asked, his curiosity growing to a keen interest. Now this was surely something. His copper's instincts were at full throttle.

'Her throat was cut, or so it seems. I am certainly no expert on these matters,' the butler replied carefully. 'I could hardly tell my mistress as much; only that we had found Ruby dead and had buried her right away. I was going to come to you with the news of it but you beat me to it.'

MacDonald mused over this news. It was not good. 'So you buried the body,' he stated, unable to hide his disappointment. He would have liked to have got a better handle on exactly what had happened here and why, but he was not prepared to dig up bodies of dead dogs. Not just yet.

'No, sir,' the butler replied. 'I told madam that we had buried the poor pet. I did not want her to see the body as it was. You understand? She has been through so much lately. The body is here, stored in an alcove off the kitchen. Would you like to see it?'

'Yes, please.'

The butler led MacDonald through the first floor of the house, into the back area where the kitchen was located. There was a cook working in the kitchen, and she looked up angrily when she saw the two men enter, her eyes centering upon the butler. 'Will you take that out of here now; it stinks something terrible.'

'Soon,' Gerald replied. Then he asked her to leave the room.

'Hah, forced to leave me own kitchen! Why I never.'

Once the cook was gone, Gerald took MacDonald into the alcove, where a small bundle lay on a table covered with a cloth. The odor of death was strong for such a small bundle. The butler lifted the covering to reveal the remains of Ruby, a sad and dead little female Yorkshire terrier.

MacDonald moved in close and looked

over the small dog's corpse. Ruby appeared to have been a hearty and healthy dog, well-fed, and not elderly as he had at first assumed. 'How old was Ruby?'

'Three years, sir. Lady Westcott purchased her after her previous Ruby passed away — that dog was very old and had been with madam many years. This Ruby replaced that Ruby.'

'I see,' MacDonald said, his eyes looking over the corpse with his mind working feverishly.

'She was a good dog,' Gerald added with a sad frown. 'She did not deserve to end her life this way.'

MacDonald nodded. He looked over the dog carefully once again, especially the wound.

'You can see where she has been cut,' Gerald added in an effort to be helpful.

The inspector nodded again as he examined the wound. The throat had most definitely been slit with a sharp instrument, probably a knife or razor. He shook his head in utter dismay. What a waste. Why murder a little dog? Why cut its throat?

'It is terrible, sir,' Gerald said most firmly, in a manner the detective figured for the butler was as close to absolute anger as a man such as he ever attained.

'Hello! What is this?' MacDonald said sharply. He moved the head to better see what had caught his attention. Ruby's mouth and teeth were brown, covered in dried blood, but that blood did not all appear to belong to the dog.

'Sir?' Gerald asked curiously. In spite of the gruesome discovery, he was unable to look away.

'This amount of blood should not be here. And Ruby is missing some of her teeth,' MacDonald stated, showing the open mouth to the butler.

'Oh my!' Gerald blurted in disgust as he finally looked away at the ugly sight. 'Please.'

'No, you must look.'

Gerald steeled himself and looked again, then shook his head. 'She was a healthy dog, Inspector. Lady Westcott saw to that assiduously. I am sure Ruby was not missing any of her teeth. Not a one.'

'Well, she is missing three — no, four

— no, *six* of her teeth now.'

'Missing six teeth? That is impossible! I don't understand, sir.'

'Neither do I, but I can venture a guess,' MacDonald said carefully, replaying his imaginings of the scene over in his mind. 'Someone for some reason wanted — or more likely needed — to kill this little dog. You said the last time Ruby was seen, she was in the back garden?'

'Yes, sir.'

'And she was a barker?'

'Oh yes, a loud and spry one for her size.'

'Aye, makes sense then.'

'What makes sense, sir?'

MacDonald ignored the question. Instead he said, 'Take me to the place in the yard where Ruby was last seen.'

The butler nodded and escorted the inspector back through the kitchen and out into the garden behind the house. It was not overly large, being appropriate for a city home, but it was certainly large enough for a small dog to run loose in. There were tall well-manicured hedges all around them, and beyond that a high wrought-iron fence that quite effectively secured the property.

'What do you think, Inspector?' Gerald asked as he escorted the detective through the garden.

'I don't know yet. The missing teeth and the blood seem to indicate that someone — a man, and probably a fairly large man — did the deed. But why? He picked up the dog — who I believe could be a rather little ferocious creature — with the purpose of killing it. This is evidenced by the fact that little Ruby fought valiantly for her life, biting the man many times and drawing blood. In fact, Ruby bit her attacker so viciously that she sank her teeth deeply into the man's hand and would not let go — she lost six of them. Her killer must have pulled her clenched jaw off his arm or hand. But the man's other hand held a knife, and he slit the poor dog's throat. It happened very fast. Ruby put up a determined fight.'

Gerald sighed deeply. 'Madam will be pleased to hear that, at least.' He then brought the detective to a section of the garden and pointed.

'So it was here?'

'Yes, sir, behind the hedges. Ruby's body was found there by Ricardo the groundskeeper. It was the odor that caught his attention, of course. The smell was rather bad. It was also around this area that Ruby was last seen alive.'

'I see,' MacDonald replied. He carefully looked over the finely manicured grounds, the grass and leaves that made up the area surrounded by the high thick hedges. These, with the fencing, made a most effective barrier for the property — or so it would seem.

'Blood droplets here, here, and here,' MacDonald stated with a knowing nod of his head.

'Yes, I see them now too, but they are barely specks.'

'No matter; they tell us the tale began here.'

The inspector looked around further, moving into the hedges. 'These hedges are thick and high, but there is a slim open area between them and the fence. And here is a mass of blood on the ground, the spot where the deed was done. This is where Ruby was killed and the body left.'

'My God, so much blood for such a little dog,' the butler said softly, looking at the dark spot on the ground between the hedges and the fence.

'Aye, but what's this? Here we go!' MacDonald added, his excitement building. 'The bars of the fence down here have been sawed at the bottom. They have been parted, bent apart, then bent back into place, to appear untouched. This is how Ruby's killer entered the garden.'

'For what purpose?'

'To kill Ruby of course,' MacDonald said softly, twisting the long ends of his mustache slowly, thinking. 'But what was the other nefarious purpose he had in mind?'

'The *other* purpose?' Gerald echoed, fearful now.

'Is anything missing in the house — money, jewelry, any valuables?' MacDonald asked. It was the next logical question after all, but he was a bit surprised by the butler's answer.

'No, nothing at all. Nothing is missing, as far as I know, and madam has not indicated anything wrong on the premises other than Ruby having gone missing. So I do not understand.'

'I think I do. Take me to your mistress right away.'

'Of course, sir.'

4

The Problem

Gerald the butler led Inspector Mac-
Donald into Lady Westcott's bedroom.
Then he quickly left them alone and shut
the door behind him, as the detective had
asked to be alone with the lady of the
house.

The old woman looked terrible, sad
and utterly defeated. It was quite
apparent that she had taken the death of
her beloved Ruby very badly.

'She's dead, Inspector — gone from me
forever!' Lady Westcott cried.

'I am sorry, ma'am,' MacDonald told
her in a soft voice, meaning it with a
sincerity that even surprised him. He had
seen the body of the little dog; that was
not any way for such a poor creature to
meet its fate.

'You saw her?'

'Well, I — '

'Please do not lie to me, Inspector. Gerald has been a loyal retainer in this family since before my husband and I were married. I know he told me a story that would spare me further grief. So I am asking again, you saw her?'

'Aye.'

'Tell me, please.'

'It was not pretty, madam,' MacDonald began softly. He did not want to tell the old lady the grim details, hoping to spare her their brutality, but now he realized she needed to know. She must know the truth, and in so doing perhaps she could help him solve this crime, or problem, at least. For the killing of a dog was certainly no crime, or leastways not a proper crime for the Yard. It was a ghastly event to be sure, but no crime . . . unless there was something more to it.

Lady Westcott nodded approvingly.

MacDonald continued, 'Ruby was murdered. It was done by the hand of some unknown man, but you can take some measure of pride in knowing that she fought her attacker fiercely. In fact, it is probable that she inflicted some rather nasty bites that drew blood from the hand of her killer.'

'She was always very brave,' Lady Westcott said, and her mood lightened a bit. Then she actually smiled as she reminisced: 'My Ruby would forever bark at the larger dogs in the neighborhood, and she always stood her ground with them.'

'So she was a barker?'

'She could be a handful for such a small dog, but I miss her so much. I appreciate that you told me the truth about this matter, and I am pleased that she fought so well. So bravely. Ruby was always a fighter. So you say she inflicted some damage upon the hand of her killer?'

'Yes, it would appear so,' MacDonald replied. 'That is also why, with your permission, I would like to question and examine all the members of your household staff immediately.'

'Of course, Inspector,' Lady Westcott agreed. Then she looked closely at the detective. 'Do you really think that one of my own people . . . ?'

'Not really, but I need to rule them out first,' MacDonald explained.

'I see.' The old woman allowed a sigh of relief.

'The bigger problem — the real problem, as I see it — is the reason why Ruby was killed. It was obviously to keep her quiet. You see, I discovered an opening in your fence in the back garden, where some unknown intruder entered the yard and killed Ruby. I am certain he did it because she would have alerted the entire household were he to enter the garden. So he had to take care of the little dog first.'

'That is terrible!'

'Yes, well, my concern now is that this person is still at large and may come back. Without Ruby on guard, he may feel he can enter your grounds — and hence the house — with impunity, then perform God knows what mischief.'

'Oh, my!'

'I don't want to alarm you at a time like this, but it is best that you and your staff remain vigilant.'

'Is there anything the Metropolitan Police can do?'

'Certainly. I will see to it that a bobby is posted at your front door and another man in your back garden along the opening in your fence. With any luck, we will catch the blighter before he causes you any more trouble.'

'Thank you, Inspector. Do you think the man is a thief, some kind of burglar?'

'More than likely. Do you keep many valuables in the house?'

'Oh yes — my diamonds, rubies, sapphires; so much gold and jewelry . . . You see, Simon always bought me the most extravagant baubles. I never cared for such flummery, but it made him happy to give them as gifts, so they do have great sentimental value to me. Actually, much of the jewelry is far too ostentatious for my taste. I never wear it anymore.

'I do not mind telling you that Simon was in some ways a commoner, even though he was from a quality family and a high lord. He had a common touch that I appreciated. A down-to-earth man, he was. I have always felt it best to put forth a demure appearance in all things, if possible. Or at least I did while Simon was alive, back in the day of the queen's ascension in '37. Back then Simon and I lived quietly in Germany. We only moved here to London 20 years ago when Simon had this house built for me. He would gift me the most extravagant jewelry for my birthday and at Christmas. Now I am afraid all those priceless baubles are gathering dust or lying about neglected in various drawers in my armoire.'

Alex MacDonald could barely believe what he was hearing. He concentrated on what he termed 'the swag'. He asked Lady Westcott if he could view her jewelry and she agreed. It was all in the room with her in various drawers and upon her dressing table, and she gathered it all together for him. It made quite the glittering pile. Once he looked over the 'loot', as he knew any burglar would see it, he whistled loudly. If it was all real — and he was certain that it was — it was a king's ransom. He could not believe it was all just sitting around in various cubbyholes and upon the top of the dresser in the lady's bedroom. He quickly gathered it all up into a large case.

'You have a fortune here in diamonds and jewelry, Lady Westcott. These need to be placed in the vault of your bank straight away for protection. Do you have someone you can trust to take these to the bank for safekeeping?'

'Gerald is completely trustworthy, Inspector.'

'Aye, then you should ring for him and tell him what to do with this treasure. I will, of course, accompany him to the bank tomorrow morning for his personal safety. Then we need to keep a lookout to be sure Ruby's killer does not return.'

'So you think the man is after my jewels?' Lady Westcott asked the inspector in evident surprise. 'I hardly care about the silly old things anymore — apart from the fact that they were gifts to me from Simon, of course. I could not stand to know that they were the reason my poor little Ruby was killed. Now Ruby is gone, and Simon as well. I am so alone.'

'I am here with you, Lady Westcott,' MacDonald said firmly, a bit surprised about his feelings of sympathy for the old woman. 'We shall ride this situation out together.'

'Thank you so very much, Inspector MacDonald.'

The young police detective's dour look softened, and he smiled. He was beginning to really like the old lady.

★　★　★

That evening, MacDonald saw to it that two stalwart London bobbies were placed on guard at the Westcott residence overnight. Before he left the house, he examined the hands of every member of the Westcott household. All passed; no one had any bite or teeth marks on their hands or arms. He had expected as much, and Lady Westcott was relieved to hear the news that none of her trusted and long-time staff were involved in this unsavory matter. However, that knowledge did not bring MacDonald any closer to solving the problem.

★　★　★

The next morning, when MacDonald relieved the two bobbies, they reported no unusual incidents overnight. The inspector was satisfied. The thief, or whoever he was, most probably had given up on his plan now that the police were seen to be on guard.

Later that morning, MacDonald accompanied Gerald to Lloyd's Bank, where Lady Westcott's jewels were deposited for safekeeping. When he returned to the Westcott residence with the butler, a hysterical maid came running down the stairway screaming at them, 'My God! My God!'

'Maria!' the butler said sharply, surprised by the young woman's behavior, and a bit angry at her excitable manner. 'Contain yourself, please! What is the meaning of this?'

'What has happened?' MacDonald asked, more to the point.

'My lady, my lady . . . She is . . . she is — gone!'

'Gone?' MacDonald repeated in surprise.

Maria wept, obviously overcome with

grief at what she had discovered.

MacDonald looked over at the butler, Gerald, and was alarmed to see a great sadness spread across the man's usually stoic face. He was obviously severely affected by this terrible news. In fact, the inspector noticed, he evidenced a sadness far deeper than anything usually shown by any mere servant to a mistress.

'She is gone?' Gerald whispered in disbelief. 'It cannot be! Oh, my dear God!'

'I am sorry,' MacDonald said softly to the butler. The hard-nosed London detective had grown to like the old woman and felt sorry at this news of her sudden demise. She was elderly and ill, so this was not any great surprise at all, but it was an upsetting turn of events.

The maid was still weeping, while Gerald was beside himself with grief as well. Ah, MacDonald thought, well that clinched it then — surely there was some manifestation of love between the butler and Lady Westcott. He could see it plainly now in Gerald's features and behavior. It was surely something much deeper than the usual loyalty of an old family retainer and his mistress. The inspector realized that Gerald had been in some sort of relationship with Lady Westcott, and he wondered if the feeling was reciprocated. But while it seemed most interesting, was it relevant? The inspector put the information aside for the moment, as there were more immediate matters to take care of.

MacDonald struggled to calm down the maid so he could question her, even as he noticed the butler fighting to gain control over his own surging emotions. He was tearful and quite distraught. It was terrible news, but the inspector wanted to investigate the matter right away.

He spoke respectfully in a low tone: 'Of course, I will need to view the body as soon as possible.'

'View the body?' Gerald whispered with some alarm. 'My lady is gone. Let her rest in peace. Please.'

'I understand,' MacDonald said softly, then added, 'But viewing her body may allow me to determine if the cause of her death was through natural causes or some form of foul play. Remember, the killing of Ruby indicates there was an intruder upon the grounds.'

Gerald thought that over for a moment, then reluctantly nodded as the maid continued to tug imploringly at his sleeve. Her action was growing more frantic by the moment and was severely annoying the butler.

'Inspector, I understand — ' Gerald began, but then stopped his words. Maria would not restrain herself at all now. Suddenly interrupted again, Gerald turned towards her and, with a harsh withering gaze, indicated he did not appreciate staff who did not know their proper place — especially at a time like this, when a terrible tragedy had occurred. While Maria was, after all, a rather simple and common village girl who was prone to emotional outbursts, Gerald had no time for her now. He shot a hard look at her once again, but could see that Maria was even more adamant in gaining his attention. Finally he gave up, and barked impatiently, 'All right, all right! What is it, Maria?'

The maid looked up carefully at the faces of the butler and the police inspector. 'I am sorry, sir, I — Lady Westcott is gone, but . . . '

'We know,' Gerald added more gently. The poor girl was distraught, near panic. Maria shook her head, more frantic and insistent than ever now. 'No! No, sir, you do not understand. I did not explain myself properly. My lady is *gone*. She is *not* dead! She is just *gone*!'

'You mean missing?' Inspector Mac-Donald said, and the butler and he looked at each other in surprise as Maria nodded frantically. Then both men instantly raced up the stairway to the old woman's bedroom.

What they found when they entered the bedchamber was just as Maria the maid had told them. Lady Westcott was gone. Her bed was empty and there was no sign of her anywhere.

'What the deuce?' Inspector Mac blurted in surprise. Where was she?

'My God! How could this happen?' the butler demanded of Maria. 'You were watching her, were you not? What did you see? Where is our lady?'

'Sir, I do not know, I swear. I came up here moments before you and the inspector returned from the bank, and I discovered my lady was missing. I called her name, but there was no response.'

'You saw no one in the house?' MacDonald demanded of the maid. 'No one who does not belong here?'

'No, sir,' Maria stammered fearfully.

'Could she have wandered off on her own?' MacDonald asked the butler.

'No sir, that's not possible,' Gerald replied in obvious shock at the very thought.

MacDonald nodded and began to look around the room. The windows were shut, with heavy drapes covering them. The room was entirely empty. He checked the large walk-in closet, full of Lady Westcott's clothing, but it too was empty of any body.

'Gerald,' MacDonald said to the butler, 'have Maria assemble the entire household staff in the library downstairs immediately. I want you to search the house for Lady Westcott. I shall join you in the search presently.'

'Yes, sir,' Gerald said, and with a nod to Maria the two of them were off, leaving the inspector alone in Lady Westcott's bedroom.

MacDonald took one more careful look around the room, with particular attention to the bed and the bedclothes — blankets, sheets, pillows. Nothing seemed out of order. There was no blood in evidence, thank God. There could have been a minor struggle by the way things were disheveled — one pillow lay upon the floor — or it could have just been the natural state of the woman's sleeping arrangements. Disheveled blankets and pillows obviously kicked around by the woman in a fitful sleep, perhaps.

MacDonald wondered what Sherlock Holmes would make of this. The old woman was missing, but she could not have disappeared into thin air as it appeared she had done. She could not have gone far, not on her own, as she was an elderly and ill woman. To take the lady from her home unseen would involve considerable resources. This appeared to be some kind of an abduction; what the Yanks called a kidnapping. MacDonald considered the possibility of an inside job; but while the abductor might have had help from someone here on the staff, or newly placed on the staff, the murder of Ruby and the hole in the garden fence, when added to the equation, bothered him very much. There was more than met the eye here, and that certainly indicated an outside agency.

MacDonald decided there was nothing more to discover in the bedroom, so he made his way quickly down the stairway and outside the house to talk to the two bobbies who were still on guard in the front and rear of the home. Neither had seen anything. He thought that most unusual and he questioned them more closely, but there was nothing to be learned from either man. Then Mac-Donald went into the library, where he saw the household staff gathered and mumbling among themselves in rabid consternation.

'Can I have your attention?' MacDonald spoke up in a firm tone.

'Give the inspector your attention now!' the butler ordered the staff. There were three maids, two cooks, a groom, a gardener and his son, and a driver, all nine members of the staff, plus the butler, Gerald.

MacDonald called to Gerald: 'Is this the entire staff?'

'Yes, sir.'

'Is anyone missing?'

'No, sir.'

MacDonald nodded. He had rather expected that to have someone missing at this point would have been too easy. Well at least that was settled. 'All right then, let's continue. Is any member of the staff a newly hired person?'

The butler looked around at the faces of his staff and gave a quick nod. 'Jenkins there, the groom, is not new, but recent.'

'Recent?'

'Yes; he came to us four years ago, but he had fine references from the Baskerville family, I can assure you.'

Inspector Alec MacDonald's dour face twisted into a grimace. Quite amazing, he thought, that four years' employment was considered as 'recent' in this household. 'That is quite sufficient.'

'Anything else, sir?'

'Yes, there is. Have there been any visitors last night or this morning? Has there been any pickup or delivery of large boxes or crates — especially early today, this morning?' MacDonald had already questioned his men stationed outside of the house, but now he needed to question the staff as well.

'No, sir.'

'Are you sure?'

'Absolutely, sir,' the butler said, and each staff member nodded their head in agreement.

'All right.' MacDonald nodded. 'I want you to organize a search of the house and grounds from basement to attic. Send the maid to the local constable to have this reported to the police immediately.'

'Yes, sir. And if I might be so bold, what are you going to do, Inspector?'

'I am going to take another look at that hole in the garden fence and see if I can track down Lady Westcott.'

5

The Search for Lady Westcott

The house was in an uproar. The deepest, darkest places were checked and rechecked, but there was no sign of the missing mistress of the house.

Inspector MacDonald did not like the looks of this case at all. Why abduct an old woman? It was evident to him now that it was not about her jewels, even though they were worth a fortune that no common criminal would ever ignore. Yet it appeared they *had* been ignored. It was most unusual.

Hence, these were not common criminals. MacDonald turned the thought over in his mind and wondered what Sherlock Holmes would make of this situation. The inspector thought of bringing the case to the attention of his friend and mentor, but he knew he needed to ascertain some additional details before he could consider such a drastic step. Holmes was a man who desired cold hard facts, and Mac-Donald knew he needed to gather many more facts than the meager amount he had now. He actually knew very little of just what exactly was going on here. And all the time the thought nagged at the back of his mind — where was Lady West-cott?

MacDonald had immediately raced to the back garden of the house to run another check on things there. He entered the spot behind the hedges where the little dog Ruby had been killed, and the place where the wrought-iron fence had been breached. He thought this must be where she had been taken away. But at a glance he realized it did not seem to be a large enough breach. While certainly big enough for a man, or men, it was most definitely not large enough for a stout woman the size of Lady Westcott. He was sure that her girth would never allow her to fit through the breach. Now that seemed to change everything. But what on earth did it mean? MacDonald thought it through carefully, rearranging his working theory once again. His thoughts on the matter startled him in surprise. What this information told him quite plainly was that Lady Westcott had not been taken away from the property in this manner. He found that perplexing but interesting. All right, then, so just how had she been abducted?

MacDonald now found himself in quite the quandary. Something was badly amiss here. The staff seemed loyal, there had been no pickup of any large box or crate that day, and the intruder did not seem to be after any jewels — but had in fact seemed to have been after Lady Westcott herself! It seemed incredible, but the facts pointed in that direction. But why abduct the old lady? Ransom? Who would pay? The thought perplexed MacDonald and was beginning to irritate him immensely. So where was the old girl? She was stout in size, aged and ill; certainly not someone to be involved in some convoluted disappearance act. He considered the idea that she had to be on the grounds of this house somewhere — but a full and detailed search by himself and the staff had discovered nothing. There was no sign of Lady Westcott.

Inspector MacDonald sighed as he realized he was at an impasse. Was it indeed time to call in Sherlock Holmes? He hesitated to disturb the great detective with what surely must be a rather trivial case; trivial in the sense that he must be missing something so obvious that Holmes would point it out to him almost immediately, to his utter embarrassment. Lady Westcott surely had to be somewhere. But where?

What he *was* sure of was that she could not have just disappeared completely. She might yet be alive, though he feared she could be dead. Might she be in hiding, perhaps from an intruder into the house? No, his men on guard had seen no one come into or out of the house, and they were good men. Might her dead body be in the house, perhaps hidden by one or more of her killers? A good theory, but no, that could not be, because no one had come into the house.

So there was no killer. Then perhaps she had had an accident or fallen ill. That seemed possible, but the inspector admitted it was a long stretch. As yet there was no odor to give evidence to this suspicion of death. And even if this theory might be true, MacDonald knew there were ways for someone not to be found, or ways for a killer to wrap a body to disguise the odor of death, at least for a time. That might mean foul play from one of the staff then, but he had to admit it seemed unlikely. He made a mental note to bring in a police dog.

Inspector Alec MacDonald nodded to himself now, remembering two of Holmes's famed axioms: *If you eliminate the impossible, then whatever remains, however improbable, must be the truth.* And the other words that he cherished from Holmes were just as valid: *It is a capital mistake to theorize before you have all the evidence. It biases the judgment.* These were words for any detective worth his salt to live by.

MacDonald smiled, remembering how Holmes had told him once years ago: *Mr. Mac, the most practical thing that you could ever do in your life would be to shut yourself up for three months and read twelve hours a day the annals of crime. Everything comes in circles . . . The old wheel turns, and the same spoke comes up. It's all been done before, and will be again.*

MacDonald shook his head in confusion, whispering to himself softly in his thick Aberdeen accent: 'Perhaps; but not this time, Mr. Holmes, for I believe this is something new, even unique. Why on earth would a wealthy and aged heiress like Lady Westcott disappear? Could she be scared and in hiding? If so, and is fearful of some intruder, why not call in the police? She *had* called in the police for her lost dog, but *not* for the intruder. Why?'

Or, the inspector thought, changing tack entirely back now to an earlier idea, had the elderly woman simply gone somewhere in the house and had an accident — fallen, or perhaps had a heart attack? Maybe she was unable to cry out for help. That might be, but there was no evidence for this theory. No cry for help had been heard by any of the staff; and if so, she would have been found and brought aid. She would certainly have been located in their search by now.

MacDonald was stymied and knew he needed help, and he knew just where to get that help. But first he would call in more members of the Metropolitan Police and give this house a professional drubbing: re-question the staff; put a bit of pressure on them; make them talk. Especially that butler, Gerald — for MacDonald had caught the hint that he and the Lady might be closer than just friendly companions. That was interesting and may prove essential. Of course it was most unacceptable behavior for a fine lady and her butler to be having an affair, but he knew such things did happen. They happened a bit too often, in fact, and always precipitated some interesting results.

★ ★ ★

Chief Inspector Sir Charles Maine was not happy with the way this case was progressing, if it was progressing at all;

and he had his doubts about that. When MacDonald had called in to see him in his office at the Yard that morning, it had been a full week since he had taken on the case, but the inspector had little to report to his impatient superior. An army of bobbies and detectives had gone through the Westcott mansion with a fine-toothed comb and come up empty. A special police dog had been brought in and discovered nothing as well. It was most disconcerting. Worse still, the popular press now had somehow got wind of the missing grand dame and was beginning to play up the disappearance in big headlines and asking many uncomfortable questions of the police — and of Sir Charles, which made the man most uncomfortable.

'I need answers, MacDonald!' he barked impatiently.

MacDonald looked at his angry superior and said bluntly, 'I do have an answer for you — of a sort, sir.'

'Good, now you are talking! What is it?'

'Sherlock Holmes,' MacDonald said simply.

Chief Inspector Sir Charles Maine shook his head. He was not in favor of this idea at all. 'This is what you come up with!'

'He can find her if anyone can, sir.'

'Hah! I have heard of this man Holmes, of course. Lestrade sometimes mentions him. I must tell you I don't like him or what he does, insinuating himself into official police business. It is improper.'

'He is not insinuating himself when he is asked to help, sir,' MacDonald explained firmly.

'Don't take that cheeky attitude with me, Alec. I like you and I respect your talent, but you are not chief inspector here. Not yet, my lad! No, I will not have it. You will just have to bear down harder on the household staff. They must know something. Look deeper and find me some answers. You are one of my best men, MacDonald, and I expect a speedy resolution of this from you soon, or heads shall roll! And among those heads will be your own!'

Inspector MacDonald swallowed nervously but quickly nodded. 'Yes, sir, I shall do all that and more. This case will be solved.'

'Good, I am glad to hear it. Now get to it!'

MacDonald did not leave, but stood there and held his ground. 'Sir, Sherlock Holmes is certainly a curious fellow, but he has been helpful in many cases, for all of which he has taken no credit. I have noticed that he seems to insert himself into only the most singular and convoluted cases, and only when he is asked to do so. In fact, he seems to be rather keen on involvement in only those cases that offer the most difficult-to-solve crimes. These pique his interest, and I am sure that he could be of significant help to us in this matter.'

'For the love of God, I cannot see how, Alec,' Sir Charles snapped.

'Be that as it may, I would like your permission to bring him into this case. As you say, if Lady Westcott is connected to the royal family in some manner, there surely is more amiss here than meets the eye. I need not elaborate to you the implications.'

'Yes, I know them only too well. The damned press are already nosing around!'

Sir Charles growled in frustration. 'God knows what they will write. They do not care about truth at all, you know; they just want to sell papers.'

'Precisely, sir,' MacDonald prompted. He could feel the wind changing in his direction. He knew to wait patiently, say nothing more, and let his superior work it out himself and come to the conclusion he wanted him to come to.

Sir Charles Maine reluctantly nodded, finally giving in to his young colleague. 'I am not keen on this Holmes fellow at all, but if you say he can solve this case for us, then you may bring him in. We need a quick closure to assuage the voracious clamor of the press. MacDonald, the disappearance of Lady Westcott is a disaster. I am told the queen herself may make inquiries soon. I am sure you understand that when she does, I want to be able to report only good news to her majesty upon this matter.'

'Of course, sir,' MacDonald said.

'Then get this Holmes fellow on the case, *and find me some answers!*'

6

Holmes Becomes Involved

Sherlock Holmes sat comfortably in his easy chair before the fireplace at 221B Baker Street with his feet upon an ottoman, as if he had not a care in the world. He puffed away contentedly upon his meerschaum pipe as he looked up at the odd pattern of tiny paint cracks in the ceiling above his head with what appeared to be a rather intense interest.

'Whatever are you looking at, Holmes?' Doctor John Watson, his friend and biographer, asked in a bit of pique. The room was already awash with a thick cloud of pipe smoke, and the doctor was getting ready to leave his seat to open a window to let in some much-needed fresh air.

'Think, old man,' Holmes muttered softly, as though in some deep trance. 'There has been significant movement among the criminal class of London recently. I can feel it in the air. Something — something rather big — is brewing, I believe.'

'How can you tell?' Watson asked, finally able to pry open the window and bask in the cool breeze of London smog as it entered the room.

'I can tell,' Holmes responded in an aloof tone.

'Hah, now you are a Svengali?'

'Merely a conduit that upon some special occasions can connect with the greater criminal sphere.'

'I do not understand what you are talking about, Holmes.'

'Of course, but it is of no consequence.'

'And, by the way, what do you find so fascinating in our ceiling? Do we have a roof leak? You have been staring up at it for the last half hour as if transfixed. I worry about you sometimes, Holmes.'

Sherlock Holmes laughed but did not reply.

Watson just shook his head. He felt this type of enigmatic behavior most vexing. 'Well? What do you see there?' Watson insisted, hoping that his friend had not once more succumbed to the call of the cocaine needle without his knowing of it and that he was even now in some deep drug-induced fugue.

'Just patterns,' Holmes answered.

'Patterns?'

'Yes, Watson, patterns. They are all around us. All we have to do is but notice them.'

'I see nothing in the ceiling at all, certainly no pattern; just a few flecks of peeling paint, a bit of dust and some spider webs in the corner. I shall have to alert Mrs. Hudson to have them cleaned, but that is all.'

'Yes, but it is not the fact of what the patterns tell us this time, for these tell us nothing. What is important is the reminder that patterns *do* exist,' Holmes stated almost mystically, now turning his gaze from the ceiling to look squarely upon Watson. 'Something, my friend, is in the works, and I have a feeling we shall be hearing of it soon.'

'You do say?'

'Yes I do.'

'Well, then it will be a welcome case and an improvement from your smoking up our rooms and staring up at the ceiling like some Hindu fakir.'

Sherlock Holmes laughed good-naturedly. 'Ah, Watson, you put it all quite succinctly.'

'Well, thank you, Holmes.'

'Hello! We have a visitor!'

'A visitor, at this hour?'

'Yes, and one from Scotland Yard, no doubt.'

'You mean Lestrade?'

'Oh no, this is much more serious. If I am not mistaken, it will be none other than Inspector Alec MacDonald; and judging by his footfalls on our steps outside our rooms, he comes here in a rush with something that may be unique. The game is afoot, Watson! Now please let the inspector in.'

'What? But there's no one — '

Suddenly there was a knock upon the door. It was Mrs. Hudson who was discovered framed in the doorway to the sitting room of the great detective when Watson answered the knock, but he could see Inspector Alec MacDonald standing patiently behind their landlady, anxious to enter and apparently with much to say.

'I am sorry, Doctor, Mr. Holmes, but the inspector here was quite insistent that he see you right away,' Mrs. Hudson stated, a bit ruffled at the suddenness of the visit.

Sherlock Holmes nodded. 'Of course, Mrs. Hudson. Please let him in.'

Scotland Yard Inspector Alec Mac-Donald entered the sitting room and gave both men a dour and business-like nod of his head. He had not much changed since Watson had last seen him in that ghastly business out at Brilstone Manor House he had chronicled as 'The Valley of Fear', but which Holmes was loath to have him publish for the foreseeable future. What a convoluted tale that had been! And now Mr. Mac, as Holmes was fond of calling him, was back with some new problem, it seemed.

'Please come in, Mr. Mac,' Holmes spoke up in a more cheery tone, for he liked this police detective — a most talented fellow — and he knew that a visit from him might precipitate a challenging

81

case. 'That will be all, Mrs. Hudson.'

Watson took the inspector's coat as Holmes said, 'From the look of things, I am sure the inspector has a most interesting tale to tell us.'

'That I do, Mr. Holmes,' said Mac-Donald as he sat down in the chair indicated by the detective, 'and I am in need of your help on this one.'

'Well certainly. Watson and I are at your disposal.'

'Thank you, Mr. Holmes.'

'Think nothing of it. Make yourself comfortable. Watson, please be so kind as to give the inspector a glass of some of that passable brandy you always foist upon our visitors. Now, Mr. Mac, begin your story and leave out nothing, no matter how trivial.'

'Aye, Mr. Holmes. I am aware of your methods, and often use them myself when I can. This time I think I have a real corker for you!'

'Excellent! Then begin when you are ready.'

MacDonald calmly and carefully went through the facts of the case as he knew them up to that moment, occasionally pausing to take a sip of brandy. Holmes listened intently without interruption. When MacDonald was finished with his narration, the great detective sat quietly for some time before speaking.

'Well, it is a conundrum for sure, but not one without certain aspects that appeal to me, and not one that is unsolvable,' Holmes stated after the inspector had gone over every fact in a detailed timeline of the disappearance of Lady Westcott, from his first meeting with her over the loss of her little dog, Ruby, to her empty bed and abduction.

'Possible abduction, you say?' Holmes noted carefully. 'Well, we must not get too ahead of ourselves here, Mr. Mac.'

MacDonald nodded. 'Of course. Actually, I suppose you are correct, Mr. Holmes, but I find myself at an impasse. My superior, Sir Charles Maine, expects results right away. The press is already leading with the story, and who knows where their inquiries will end up. At first I supposed the old girl was the dowager of some obscure noble house and there would be no serious press interest other than the usual. We can handle that. However, I have now been informed that Lady Westcott is related somehow to the royal family, and — '

'You need say no more; I fully understand the implications,' Holmes replied with a wry grin. 'You do realize that Lady Westcott is more than just someone *related* to the royals? Though this is not generally known, and I imagine even kept very secret, she is the older sister of the queen.'

'Older sister? I had no idea!' MacDonald stated in evident surprise.

'Few are aware of the fact,' Holmes stated.

'That's preposterous, Holmes!' Watson stammered in shock. 'How can our good queen have an *older* sister? Why, that would mean that being the older sister, she would be first in line to be . . . queen!'

'Yes. It is a deep and dark family secret, and I can assure you it is never spoken of. Lady Westcott herself vehemently denies it, of course. The palace does as well.'

'How can this be?' Watson blurted, still astounded by the implications of such knowledge. He was well aware of what an older sibling of the queen might mean to the present queen's claim to the throne.

Holmes smiled indulgently. 'Families have many secrets, and a special dynamic all of their own. Royal families have them as well, but at an exalted level.'

'But Holmes!' Watson stammered in awe. 'If this is true, it could change everything!'

'Indeed, my friend.'

Watson was stunned by this information, and looked over to Inspector MacDonald to see that the police detective was in utter shock as well. He looked at Holmes questioningly. 'But how do you know this?'

'My brother Mycroft mentioned it once to me long ago, very much on the hush-hush of course. And I expect you both will keep silent about what I have just told you as well.'

'Of course, Holmes,' Watson said softly, taking in this information and what it might mean — that their good Queen

Victoria had somehow usurped the throne from her rightful older sister! It was astonishing! Worse yet, it could plunge the nation — the very empire — into chaos or civil war!

Sherlock Holmes looked inquiringly at the Scotland Yard detective.

'Yes, for sure, I'll utter not a word,' MacDonald added quickly. Then he looked closely at the great detective. 'But what does it all mean — her going missing, I mean?'

'Ah, that has yet to show itself; but there is one fact I can tell you for certain.'

'And what might that be?' MacDonald asked, grasping for any informational life-line Holmes might offer.

'The woman's location. Of course you know, Mr. Mac, that Lady Westcott has never left her home at all, and that she is hiding somewhere in that vast mansion.'

Inspector MacDonald took a deep breath of resignation as his fingers twisted the ends of his long, bushy mustache. 'I don't understand. I mean, I have looked, and I have looked *hard*, I assure you! I have had constables, the police, even the household staff search everywhere, but the woman is not to be found. Short of tearing down the entire building, a massive and time-consuming undertaking in such a huge mansion, there is no way to find her.'

'Especially if, as I surmise for some unsuspected reason, she does not want to be found,' Holmes stated with a sly grin.

'You think she could be . . . hiding? From what? I do not understand,' MacDonald asked in surprise. 'That puts an entirely different aspect to this business. So what do I do?'

'That is a good question,' Holmes replied with a sharp look. 'The intruder into this house is real, and she knows about him — she knows who he is and what he wants. She knew it since her little dog was found dead. She is petrified of what it means. But what does it mean?'

'Yes, what does it mean, Holmes?' Watson asked anxiously.

Holmes stood by for a long moment, thinking silently.

Watson was nearly frantic. 'This could bring down the monarchy!'

'It is serious,' Sherlock Holmes replied calmly. 'Remember what I told you about unintended consequences, Watson? Well, now that fact of her being the older sister of our good Queen Victoria could change the entire game. However, it may also be the key to us unlocking this problem. Mr. Mac, I need to make certain inquiries first, and then Watson and I shall meet you at Lady Westcott's home tomorrow precisely at noon. Then hopefully we will be able to clear this matter up once and for all.'

Inspector MacDonald nodded with evident relief that his friend, Mr. Holmes, was now on the case. He arose from his seat and shook hands with Sherlock Holmes and Doctor Watson. 'Very well, gentlemen. Until tomorrow at noon.'

7

The Missing Lady Anne

Once Inspector MacDonald was gone from the building, Sherlock Holmes spoke to Watson in a soft whisper.

'An interesting and dangerous situation is brewing, with a missing woman who I believe does not want to be found. There is that on the one hand. On the other hand, she is the older sister of our very own good Queen Vic, and that means problems in the monarchy, as I am sure you understand, Watson.'

'I had no awareness of her, Holmes. None at all.'

'Nor does 99.99 percent of the population of Britain. Lady Anne's sisterhood to the queen has been kept a jealously guarded secret for decades, and over that time it has been, thankfully for all concerned, forgotten. She has never acknowledged it.'

'But why, Holmes? She might have become the queen of Britain.'

'There are complications, Watson,' Holmes stated enigmatically, but he would not explain further just yet, and Watson knew better than to press his companion for facts he was not yet ready to divulge.

Watson sighed in resignation. 'Yes, it must be complicated. It does remind me a bit of the disappearance of Lady Frances Carfax, does it not, Holmes?'

'This is serious business indeed. We must first learn if she has joined the plot, or is being held by persons unknown,' Holmes stated firmly.

'Joined the plot? Whatever do you mean? What plot?'

'Why, the plot to murder Queen Victoria and have her replaced with her older sister, of course, which would make Lady Anne Westcott Queen Anne of England. That plot, Watson.'

'Holmes?' Watson inquired softly.

'Yes, my friend?'

'Are you serious? This surely cannot be! It is a bare two years since the celebration of Queen Victoria's Golden Jubilee — 50 years of her glorious reign. She is a very popular monarch.'

'I have never been more serious,' Sherlock Holmes stated firmly. 'Now if you will excuse me, I must get dressed.'

'Dressed? Wherever are you going at this time of night?'

'To the Diogenes Club to see Mycroft. If I hurry, I'll get there before they close the Stranger's Room for the day.'

'I see,' Watson said softly, a bit chagrined that Holmes had not invited him to come along with him as usual. 'And what am I to do in the meantime?'

'Buck up, Watson; you have an important task that needs to be done.'

'I do?'

'Certainly, and there is no one else I would trust more than you to do it. You are to remain here at our headquarters and await the delivery of certain very important messages I shall be expecting.'

'Messages? Messages from whom?'

'Oh, from various of my agents, old man. You see, I will soon set in motion certain queries, and the results of them will be sent here. I'm afraid you may find yourself up all night, for you shall be receiving telegrams and hand-delivered letters at all hours of the evening and into the early morning. Sorry for the inconvenience, my friend. Of course most of these queries will not bear fruit at all, I am afraid; but even if only one of them does, then we are in the game! Are you up for it?'

'Of course, Holmes. You know I would do anything I can for you. Thank you for putting your trust in me in this matter.'

'Hah, Watson, there is no one I trust more! Now, let me get dressed; I have a lot to do and a short time in which to do it. I'm afraid we will each have a long night tonight. I shall not see you again until late tomorrow morning, when I will meet you here. Then we shall leave Baker Street and go together to meet Mr. Mac at the residence of Lady Westcott and settle this matter for good or ill.'

'I see. Well then, good luck, Holmes, and please be careful.'

'Tut tut, old man, I am always careful. I shall see you here bright and early tomorrow morning. Remember, collect and save all messages, no matter how obscure or obtuse they may appear to be. I want you to read them all, but save everything for my later inspection. That includes any envelopes.'

'Yes, Holmes, of course,' Watson replied with a firm nod of his head.

'Then I am off! As Herr Mozart so adequately put it, it is time for a little night music, my friend.' And with those words, Sherlock Holmes rushed into his room, where he made much noise. After many moments he rushed out of his room fully dressed, this time as a common laborer holding a handful of what appeared to be quickly scribbled letters. Then he was out the door in a flash, gone without another word.

8

Eine Kline Nachtmusik

No sooner had Sherlock Holmes exited 221 Baker Street than he was met upon the front stoop of the building by a young man who had been waiting there for him eagerly.

'Sorry I took so long,' Holmes stated, handing the lad a small bundle of folded notes. Each one had a name and address written upon the outside of it.

'Why, Mr. Holmes, I'd hardly recognize you in that garb. You look like a proper working bloke now, you do. A chimney sweep, could it be?'

Holmes allowed a slim grin. 'Could be, Wiggins. An adequate deduction. Then again, a rat catcher, perhaps?'

'Surely,' the young man replied with a wide grin.

'So you know what you need do with these?' Holmes asked the boy.

'Aye, sir, I surely do. Me and the lads will deliver the letters straight away to all the men named at the London addresses you've written upon them.'

'Have a care; these are not the best of men our fair London has to offer. Have your lads drop off the notes and then quickly depart. The recipients will read my queries immediately and arrange to answer them in their own way and with their own people.'

'I understand. So you'll have answers in a matter of hours?'

'Not I, but poor Doctor Watson will collect the replies. Now I must be off on other matters.'

'Good luck, Mr. Holmes,' the youth said with a warm smile.

'Luck has nothing to do with it, young Wiggins,' Sherlock Holmes stated firmly, and then he was gone.

★   ★   ★

A nondescript working man made his way quickly and in evident haste. Time was of the essence and there was much to do. He walked up the steps to the front door of the venerable establishment known as the Diogenes Club. He was instantly looked upon most dubiously by Higgins, the regimented doorman who gave a singularly low-brow look of disdain. However, Higgins suddenly recognized the man when he spoke, so he held the door open and allowed the strange visitor to enter the prestigious club.

As the visitor passed through the front door, he was immediately met by the venerable butler, Mr. James-Jones, who, standing stern guard like a beefeater at the palace, looked closely at the rather rough-looking visitor with evident disapproval.

'Good evening, James-Jones,' the newcomer said in a soft but commanding voice that surprised the venerable butler.

It was *him*, James-Jones realized. The man was not dressed well at all, and certainly was wearing apparel far below his station, most unsuitable to the club. Perhaps the man was 'slumming', as the toffs called it these days. However, like Higgins, he recognized the man's voice instantly and allowed him entrance into the fine establishment without any interference.

'Mr. Holmes is waiting for you . . . Mr. Holmes,' James-Jones stated succinctly.

'Thank you,' the visitor replied with a wry grin. It was ever thus when he came to these hallowed halls to visit his elder brother.

'Follow me, sir,' the butler announced, and then put his finger to his lips to warn that from this point on not one word was to be spoken. The visitor well understood the rules of silence that were strictly enforced in the club in all but one room — the Stranger's Room, his destination.

Holmes nodded in agreement at the request as he followed James-Jones; visitors were never allowed to roam the environs of the club unescorted. The butler wove a trail through the halls of this most singular of clubs whose membership comprised what were termed the most un-clubbable men of London. First among those was his own brother.

Once escorted to the Stranger's Room, Sherlock Holmes was allowed entrance, and then the butler left the room, closing the door quietly behind him. The room was large and plush, even ornate, with carved wood beams and paneling, regal portraits upon the walls, and a long empty boardroom table in the center surrounded by heavy exquisite elegant chairs that did not look at all comfortable.

The room was presently empty. Sherlock Holmes waited patiently. The clock on the mantel of the fireplace showed one minute before the hour of ten p.m.

Precisely one minute later, the door opened, and into the room strode a large and tall gentleman in exquisite attire, much rushed and breathing heavily. He came into the room, saw his visitor, and with a nod shut the door behind him.

'Sherlock.'

'Mycroft.'

The two brothers acknowledged each other with a terse nod of the head. Each took the full measure of the other, noting all aspects of face and form of his sibling. Then it was time for what they liked best: business and cold hard facts.

Sherlock Holmes began it. 'I am curious about two Russian killers,' he stated in a dispassionate voice.

Mycroft nodded. 'Rostoff and Rutin.'

'I see. Newly arrived?'

'Barely days ago.'

'And the reason?'

'They are up to something. We have not as yet discerned their mission,' Mycroft stated.

'The fact that such deadly men are here now means there is something rather serious afoot.'

'Obviously,' the elder Holmes brother replied with a slight snicker.

'But you have no knowledge of their plan?'

'Not as yet. We are allowing them some sway, watching them quietly but closely to see what comes up.'

The younger Holmes brother allowed a coy grin. 'I should not allow them too much leeway, brother.'

'I am aware of that, Sherlock.'

'Good. And just by the by, I have it on some authority they have gone rogue and are no longer under the employ of the

Russians. They are selling their talents to the highest bidder these days. They have a new master now; a Teutonic one.'

'I see. You know something; that is why you are here.'

'Cards on the table, Mycroft?'

'Yes, by all means, cards on the table now, for I fear this matter has become quite serious,' the elder Holmes brother stated, looking at his younger sibling with a serious frown. The game was certainly afoot now, as brother Sherlock was often fond of saying. 'These Russians are highly professional assassins. Do you know who might be their target? I have a suspicion who may be pulling their strings.'

Then the Holmes brothers each told the other of what they knew of the situation, each one intersecting his pieces of the puzzle and facts with what the other knew. The picture that emerged was quite alarming.

After they spoke, Sherlock Holmes left his elder brother and the Diogenes Club. His next stop was the British Royal Library. It was well after midnight when he arrived, and the British Royal Library was closed for the evening, but the man dressed as a common workman walked boldly up the granite steps towards the elegant front entrance. That too was closed and locked shut, but the guard on duty there noticed the strange man walking towards him and placed a cautionary hand upon his truncheon in case of any trouble as the newcomer approached.

'The library is closed. Now you'd best be off and away from here!' the guard warned. He drew his truncheon and showed it to the approaching man meaningfully.

'Why Philip Hargrove, you surely do not recognize me?'

'I recognize the voice now. Mr. Holmes, is it truly you?' the guard asked in wonderment.

'Of course it is.'

'Then come closer and be welcome, and let me have a look at you.'

Holmes approached Hargrove, and the guard put away his truncheon and now smiled as he marveled at the appearance of the man before him. 'Why, I never seen the likes. You look like any proper sweep or street hawker, Mr. Holmes. Surely you do! So you're in disguise, I take it?'

'Yes, Mr. Hargrove,' Holmes replied.

Hargrove nodded conspiratorially, then whispered, 'Not one word shall escape me lips about this, I promise. Now how can I be of assistance?'

'I need access to the library in order to look up certain records. Would you be able to allow me the run of the place for a few hours?'

'For you, Mr. Holmes? Why certainly,' Hargrove said, in awe at the thought of being of assistance in one of the great detective's cases. He quickly took his master key and unlocked the main entrance to the library, allowing Holmes inside. 'Just yell if you need anything, sir. I'll be right out here. Take your time; we have all night, and I do not get off duty until six in the morning.'

'Thank you, Mr. Hargrove.'

'My pleasure, Mr. Holmes. I hope you find what you're looking for.'

'I hope so too,' Holmes said as he entered the staid and stolid institution that was the British Royal Library. He went to work immediately.

★ ★ ★

The Embassy of The German Empire was located on a well-guarded estate carved out of a wealthy corner of London. It was walled off with pointed wrought-iron bars, and there were vicious guard dogs inside the compound before one ever could get to the residence of the ambassador.

Sherlock Holmes was now on the grounds surrounded by absolute darkness, unseen, undetected. The guard dogs did not catch his scent, nor were the armed men on round-the-clock guard duty aware of his presence. Holmes could be like a shadow when he did not want to be seen. He used that shadow method now as he silently trod the empty halls of the ambassadorial residence on the third floor of the building to confront the man who was behind the plot.

His Royal Highness, Prince Johan Gotha-Coburg, Ambassador of the German Empire to the British Empire, was reading a group of reports in his private residence when the detective walked in and boldly confronted him.

'Please do not get out of your chair,' Holmes ordered. 'We need to talk privately.'

The ambassador did as he was told for the moment, remaining silent and motionless, utterly shocked and surprised by the sudden chilling voice of this intruder into his most private residence. How had the man got in here?

'Who are you? What are you doing here? I shall call the guards immediately!' the ambassador threatened sternly as he saw the strange dark figure approach him out of the shadows of his room. At first he thought it might be some assassination attempt, but something about the look of the man and his stated need for a private talk seemed to belie that. There was also something about the appearance of this man in his private rooms that held him back from calling for the guards, at least for the moment. Curiosity had him in its power. Perhaps this was one of his own many spies making some important personal report; such things were not uncommon in his line of work.

The ambassador took a deep breath and then spoke softly, 'Go on, I am listening.'

'I am Sherlock Holmes, a consulting detective,' the stranger said matter-of-factly; though now that the man had moved closer into the light of his lamp, the ambassador saw that his visitor appeared to be nothing more than a common British laborer. Of course, the ambassador knew that in his line of work appearances were often deceiving and initially meant little, if nothing. The man was obviously in some sort of disguise.

'I have heard of you, Mr. Holmes. What do you want of me?'

'Only to warn you off unofficially, you understand.'

'Warn me off?'

'Lady Anne Westcott.'

'Ah yes, you mean the future Queen Anne,' the ambassador said with a growing smile of satisfaction. It was one of his latest schemes to disrupt the empire that he loathed.

'That will never happen. She will never cooperate with you and your plan.'

'We have our ways, I assure you. She is German, after all. She will come to see reason eventually, Mr. Holmes. She is my great-aunt. Family bonds tug hard upon her, and so does her love of the Fatherland, even though her mind has become somewhat tainted by her life here in London.'

'No, I am afraid it is you who must come to reason, sir, and cease this adventurism immediately. And I see you have a bandage upon your arm. May I ask how you obtained the injury?'

'You may well ask,' the ambassador stated, but he remained silent upon the matter.

'Then that is all I need know. Have a pleasant evening, Ambassador.' Then Sherlock Holmes blended back into the shadows of the room to disappear from sight and was soon gone. Though the alarm was sounded and guards and dogs were brought in, the intruder was not to be found. The ambassador's visitor had melted into the night and was gone.

It was now early morning, the sun was up, and the people of London were beginning to go about their daily lives and business. The laborer in working attire and carrying a sack of small wooden cages, poles, traps and other accoutrements of his trade knocked loudly upon the front door of the house on Abercrombie Road. The mansion was certainly large and impressive, and the visitor looked it over with a careful eye.

It was a full minute before an immaculately liveried butler answered the call and opened the door to look down his nose disapprovingly at the rough visitor who was there so early in the morning. 'The tradesmen's entrance is in the rear, my good man,' was all he said as he made ready to shut the door.

The visitor deftly stuck his foot forward, blocking the door from closing, as he muttered firmly, 'Rats is what I'm 'ere for, good sir! Big 'airy dangerous rats overrunning the neighborhood. I been sent 'ere by the city to catch 'em. You 'ave lots of 'em 'ere, sir. They're all over the city now — why, they're big enough to eat a small dog!'

The butler blanched in dire dismay, horrified. 'Rats, you say?'

'Aye, good sir. Big 'airy 'ungry ones. All over, they are. I been sent to examine each of the 'omes of the quality to protect 'em from the infestation. May I come in to do my job?'

The butler had never heard of such a thing, but he knew about rats from his childhood growing up as a poor boy in London and he shuddered. An 'infestation' of all things — good God! He nodded eagerly. 'Yes, by all means, come in. Do your job. What do you need?'

'Nothing much, good sir. I just gots to check your attic and basement. Will that be allowed?'

'Yes, certainly. But please do so quietly, and do not tell any of the staff your reason for being here.'

The visitor gave the butler an exaggerated wink to acknowledge that he would keep the secret just between them.

'And please, before you leave, let me

know if you see any signs of rats. Please.'

'Will do, good sir. I'll be on the lookout for droppings, nests, other sign you know, and I promise to be as quiet as a mouse.'

'Then follow me,' the butler said as he shook his head sadly. Rats! Imagine that, and in this part of London! It was unthinkable, but he allowed the rat chaser into the house and took him to where he wanted to go. He only hoped word of this dismal situation would not get out before it was cleaned up.

9

A Long, Strange Night

Watson shook his head in astonishment at Holmes's strange and enigmatic ways. He now found himself alone in their sitting room, seated in his chair and enjoying a long smoke of his pipe, the air now more breathable without the constant fug of his friend's overpowering tobacco smoke. He was trying to relax, attempting to get through reading a recent biography of General Gordon and his travails against the Mahdi in Khartoum in 1885.

Watson was just about to doze off, and the heavy volume had slipped from his hands, when he was alerted to the first of many visitors to come to 221B that long evening. The fellow was a special courier with a sealed letter which he hand-delivered to the doctor. Watson signed the receipt, then quickly showed the messenger out and placed the letter upon the breakfast table. He would read it later. Soon thereafter, more telegrams were delivered which Watson had to sign for. These too he placed upon the table. A small pile was quickly forming. Then the telegrams stopped, as it was growing late in the evening. With Holmes out, God alone knew where, Watson now held the fort.

Things became more awkward in the middle of the night. Mrs. Hudson was fast asleep while callers continued to come knocking on the downstairs door. So as not to disturb his landlady, Watson quickly trod down the steps and opened the street door to all manner of strange fellows. These appeared to be nondescript ruffians, thugs, ne'er-do-wells, and obvious footpads — dangerous men employed on dangerous errands. None stepped inside the foyer, nor did Watson invite them inside; but each one quickly pressed a letter or folded piece of paper into the doctor's hands and then sped off. They were gone as quickly as they had arrived.

Watson read the notes and messages soon afterwards, and most seemed quite straightforward. Some just had the single word 'No' or 'Nothing' scribbled on them, while others said 'No news' or 'Sorry'. One said, 'Drop Dead!' Watson looked that one over carefully, and with unbridled anger, but he could discern no indication of the sender. He was sure Holmes would know and made a mental note to ask him later.

The worst was a cheeky fellow who pressed a crumpled scrap of paper into his hand and snickered before he left. The cheap alcohol on his breath was horrid and overpowering. Watson was glad when the man was gone and just shook his head as he quickly locked the outer door behind him and walked upstairs, where he opened up the crumpled note and read it immediately. He was most curious about this one. He adjusted the lamp light, then looked at what was written on the paper carefully.

'Hah! What's this?' he muttered out loud in surprise. He stared at the paper, then flattened it out on the breakfast table and read it out loud.

½ pint of good gin.

2 bottles of port.
1 case Russian Vodka via Germany.
And a bottle of bitter.

Watson stared at the words with confusion. 'What nonsense is this? Must be some drunkard's wish list for a bender, or maybe a shopping list for some dodgy Limehouse pub.' He shook his head, sat back down, and promptly fell asleep. The sun was just coming up on a new day, but there were no more visitors or messages.

10

Baker Street

Sherlock Holmes arrived at Baker Street a few hours later at precisely eleven o'clock. He was dressed in the same clothing he had worn when he had left the night before upon his secret mission. It was obvious to the doctor that he had been up all night, but he appeared none the worse for wear.

'Good to see you up and about, Watson,' the great detective stated briskly. He had a cheery attitude now that the case was moving along. 'You had quite the busy night, I see.'

'You have no idea. Callers at all hours. You were right about that,' Watson stated. 'Where do you find these fellows? They seemed a collection of the worst of unsavory ruffians. Some of them looked as if they were newly released from Dartmoor.'

'Some were.'

Watson gulped nervously.

'Did they deliver any messages that seemed important? You did read them all, as I asked?'

'Of course. They were mostly answers that were in the negative. Some of them were obviously insulting, and one did not make sense to me at all. Some cheeky fellow reeking of cheap drink gave me what I presume was a shopping list for a pub, of all things!'

'Really?'

'Yes, and a most unsavory fellow he was too.'

'I am sure he was. That must have been Bobby Blake. He does like his drink — so much so that he has made his own secret code incorporating all manner of alcoholic references. It really is quite unique.'

'A code?'

'Yes, Watson. Let me see his message.'

Watson found it upon the breakfast table and handed it to Holmes. 'It is just a crumpled piece of paper with scribbles upon it.'

'And hence a scrap of no apparent importance,' Holmes stated.

'Yes, that is what I thought at the time.'

'Which is exactly what Blake wanted it to appear to be should he be taken and the message discovered.'

'Oh. I had no idea.'

Holmes took the scrap of paper and studied it carefully, nodded, then said happily, 'Well that does it! Bobby came through.'

'He did? So what does it mean?'

The detective did not reply, but quickly and methodically went through all the other messages, papers, telegrams, and even the envelopes Watson had collected from the night before and placed on their table, then nodded. 'You were right, not much here at all, but you did well. You unerringly homed in on the one message of true merit — Bobby Blake's coded list of spirits.'

'I did? I'm afraid I don't see it, Holmes. I mean, 'Half a pint of good gin'? Really now!'

'It is not what it seems. It's all in the code. I do not have time now to go into it with you, but the meaning is clear to me. Here is the breakdown. 'Half a pint of good gin' tells me that half of the royal family will accept a new queen. I assume that is the German side of the family. 'Two bottles of port' tells me that there are two agents now in port, in London, who are here waiting and ready to perform the actual assassination. 'One case of Russian Vodka via Germany' to me seems plain enough: the plot is comprised of Russian agents, or is coming through Russia, though it was certainly hatched in Berlin. Even Mycroft agreed with me on this point.'

'I see, Holmes. It is quite convoluted.'

'And meant to be so.'

'So what of the last part, 'And a bottle of bitter'?'

'Ah, yes. It will all be made to look like an accident, my friend, the assassination of good Queen Victoria — but only when a suitable replacement can be made to cooperate with the plotters.'

'Replace the queen? You mean with Lady Westcott?'

'Yes; but you see, there is a major problem. Lady Westcott has not cooperated. She has either absconded, or is in hiding — as I believe, or has staged an abduction herself!'

117

'Are you sure?'

'At least it is a working premise. But it is not what you may think, Watson. We have much more yet to discover. Did you know that there have been many attempts to assassinate the queen? This has been a real problem since the beginning of her reign. These days we take it for granted that our popular queen has no enemies, but power always attracts the worst sorts of people,' Holmes stated as he went into his room, took off his worker's clothes and quickly changed into his normal clothing. In a few moments he came back into the sitting room, now dressed in his usual attire and ready to go.

'But where is she being held? Surely not in her own home?'

Holmes adjusted his shirt collar and nodded. 'Yes, certainly. Somewhere in that vast mansion, or upon the grounds of the property, there must be a secret room — and we must find it soon. She has little time left, Watson.'

'Then we should be off.'

'Yes, at once. Inspector Mac is expecting us.'

11

Lady Westcott

At the front door of the home of Lady Westcott, Inspector Alec MacDonald patiently looked at his pocket watch to check the time. It was just shy of noon when Sherlock Holmes and Doctor Watson pulled up in a carriage and quickly joined him at the front door.

'Good to see you, Mr. Holmes, and you too, Doctor Watson,' MacDonald said in his thick Aberdeen accent, his long bushy eyebrows bristling with alert interest.

'And I you, Mr. Mac,' Holmes said quickly, shaking hands and now eager to get to work. The inspector led Holmes into the Westcott home. Watson followed behind, and soon the trio were in the large foyer, the two new visitors taking a moment to look over the details of the beautiful mansion. It was quite amazing and sumptuous. There was a large and lovely chandelier overhead in the foyer, priceless paintings upon the walls, and a long, winding, elegant staircase that led to the bedrooms upstairs. Covering the wall along the staircase were yet more exquisite paintings showing powerful men and beautiful women.

'The Westcotts, Mr. Holmes,' MacDonald stated as the men looked around in awe and deep thought.

'Is that Lord Nelson?' Watson exclaimed in surprise as he spotted one of the paintings of a naval officer who was missing an arm.

'Yes, I believe there is some relation there as well,' Holmes said matter-of-factly, though his attention was certainly off in another area entirely.

Inspector MacDonald stood quietly for the moment, allowing the detective a bit of time to absorb the layout of the house and get a feel for things there. He was very keen on this Sherlock Holmes fellow and regarded him as a genius when it came to crime. He wished he was able to see the tiny and seemingly insignificant details the man often discovered and used to close cases. And MacDonald was also quite taken with Holmes' own compliments expressed to himself as being a detective of considerable talent.

'She is here, Watson, I will swear it!' Holmes said excitedly.

'But where, Holmes?'

'Somewhere in this house, or upon the grounds, there is a secret place where Lady Westcott is hiding. I cannot say for certain yet exactly where it may be,' Holmes stated, though he was totally assured of the first part of his working theory.

'Aye, Mr. Holmes. I would be most happy with an answer to where — and then why — right now,' said MacDonald. 'I considered just such a thing straight away. However, it's not as simple as it seems. Were this one of the ancient mansions that have existed for hundreds of years that abound in England and Scotland, I would readily admit the existence of some secret room, or even rooms. Those old houses were often riddled with secret passages and hidden compartments. But the Westcott mansion was built by Lady Westcott's husband, Sir Simon, a mere 20 years ago as a gift to his wife upon their move from Berlin to London.'

'So it is not some ancient manse full of secret alcoves and mysterious medieval passageways?' Watson asked, seemingly a bit disappointed at the prospect.

'I'm afraid not, Watson,' Holmes replied with a wry grin. 'And you are quite correct, Mr. Mac, about the age of the house. But I have done some digging around myself upon the matter; last night, in fact. You see, this house was built upon the foundations of the old Seaford armory, and therein lies a secret that may answer all of our questions as to the whereabouts of Lady Westcott.'

MacDonald and Watson looked askance at the great detective, each one slowly forming words upon their lips to utter a host of questions, but Holmes cut them off.

'Not now; we have no time. We must repair to the basement,' Holmes ordered sharply. Then he was off, seemingly knowing exactly where he was going, though he had apparently never been in the house before in his life. He noted the faces of his companions when he looked back to see if they were following him, and he quickly explained, 'I studied the floor plans of the house last evening at the Royal Library.'

'Oh,' Watson stated as he and Mac-Donald struggled to keep up with their leader. 'But Holmes, the library was closed when you left Baker Street last evening.'

'Quite so, my friend, but I made a hasty unofficial visit to view the architectural floor plans. All these grand old houses have them on file there. Come now!'

The trio descended a long row of stout wooden stairs and were soon down in the dark, dank basement. MacDonald quickly struck a match and lit the lamps. They were in a large and mostly sparse space with a few items held there in abeyance, the usual and expected old furniture and storage boxes. Holmes stopped and eyed the area with sharp attention. Then he turned about and did a quick examination of the wooden stairs, taking out his magnifying glass and bending down to study the still-firm and new wood. He nodded knowingly, then put his glass away and rejoined his companions.

'You see the problem?' MacDonald said.

'Of course,' Holmes replied with an easy nod of his head.

Watson looked from one detective to the other — the official detective to the consulting detective. 'Well, I do not see it. Would either of you mind explaining to me what the problem is?'

Mr. Mac allowed a brief laugh. 'No footprints, Doctor. I came down here the first day and did the search myself, thinking it the logical place to look — here, and in the attic, of course — but I could find no evidence of anyone passing this way. There were no footprints in either location.'

Now Watson nodded in understanding. 'The floor is clean. In fact, it appears to be spotless! How can that be?'

Holmes nodded, but he continued observing the area closely, and Watson saw a wry grin cross his lips. 'You are on to something. What is it, Holmes?'

The detective nodded. 'You were right to come here, Mr. Mac, but you missed the one key piece of evidence that shows there has been a recent passage of people through here.'

'How so, Mr. Holmes? There are no footprints in the dust to see because there is not any dust!'

'A basement should have dust. A lot of dust, especially on the floor,' Watson stated, then scratched his head. 'But there is no dust anywhere — not upon the floor, but also not even upon the old furniture or the storage boxes.'

'Precisely, my friend,' said Holmes. 'The area is clean. There is no dust anywhere — no dust to allow any footprints to be discovered.'

'Ah, yes, Mr. Holmes, but don't be getting too fancy on me just yet. I did think of that,' MacDonald stated with pride as he pulled upon the end of his bushy mustache. 'I immediately called down the butler, Gerald, and put the question to him, and he explained it all to my satisfaction.'

'Really? And what did he tell you?'

Holmes asked thoughtfully, as Watson looked at his friend's stone-like face. The doctor wondered in amazement whether Holmes had made some error.

'The butler told me that Lady Westcott is a stickler for cleanliness,' MacDonald explained. 'Apparently she has always been rather obsessive in that regard. She demands clean, dust-free floors and furnishings, even up in the attic and down here in this basement.'

Holmes only cleared his throat in reply.

'So you see, we are at an impasse once again,' MacDonald offered, allowing a hint of victory to creep into his voice.

Holmes walked towards the northern wall, his fingertips feeling along the cold bricks with delicate precision. He nodded, looked sharply over at MacDonald and said, 'Mr. Mac, please go upstairs and find that butler, as well as the maid Maria you told me about — she was the one who discovered Lady Westcott missing, correct?'

'Yes she was, Mr. Holmes,' MacDonald replied. 'And Mr. Holmes, there is something else. That butler, Gerald . . . '

'Yes?' Holmes asked.

'I am sure he's in some sort of emotional relationship with Lady Westcott. There is something between them for certain. I can see he has powerful feelings for her, though he tries to hide it and would surely deny it if asked. It's something far more than the usual loyalty or fealty that a long family retainer would normally have toward his mistress.'

Holmes nodded. 'Quite so, Mr. Mac. A worthwhile observation. Please see to it that they are both brought down here forthwith.'

'Yes, Mr. Holmes. I will go myself and fetch them now.'

Once Inspector MacDonald had gone and Holmes and Watson were alone in the basement, the great detective said, 'Come now, Watson, we have little time to waste.'

'What do you mean, Holmes?'

The detective walked over to the north wall, his frenzied fingers feeling for something Watson could not see. 'Our Mr. Mac was very nearly correct. Lady Westcott saw to it that her floors were kept clean and dust free, even down here

— but it was for a far more devious reason than a mere fetish for extreme cleanliness. It was to protect the location of her secret room, should she ever have need of it.'

'I don't understand. For what purpose would she have a secret room?' Watson asked as he watched his friend deftly search the bricks of the ordinary-looking wall for something that the doctor could not see.

'There are no footprints to betray her passage here because she wanted it that way. This bolt hole was added by her late husband 20 years ago when the house was built for her protection. You see, he loved his wife dearly, but feared for her safety. History tells us that the British monarchy is replete with all manner of familial murders and devious plots, and we are neck deep in one of the worst of them now.' He let out a sudden low exclamation of triumph. 'Here we are, Watson. See this little nub of brick? Insignificant and unobtrusive, is it not?'

'I would never have noticed it. Yes, I see it, now that you point it out to me.'

Holmes smiled, then pressed the nub, or button, and the wall suddenly and silently moved sideways, revealing a large and well-appointed room. The secret room was softly lighted, carpeted and warm, and held a large table, chairs, and even an ornate and comfortable-looking bed. Lying upon that bed was an elderly woman who looked up as if startled from sleep.

'Lady Anne Westcott, I presume?' Holmes asked in a wry tone.

'What? Who are you? However did you find me, young man?' the elderly woman said in a loud and rather fearful voice.

'We will discuss that later. All you need know now is that you are safe, Lady Westcott, and the plotters have been apprehended. They shall never be allowed to reach you or impose their will upon you ever again.'

'Thank God! And who, may I ask, are you?'

'My name is Sherlock Holmes, and this gentleman is my friend, Doctor Watson.'

'Oh my God!' And the old lady suddenly swooned into a dead faint.

'Quick, Watson, see to her right away!' Holmes said immediately, but Watson was already at the woman's bedside, examining her and then helping her to regain consciousness.

'She has been under a tremendous strain, Holmes, and the shock of her discovery by us was just too much for her to take in all at once. She will come round and be fine soon.'

'Good man! She has had quite a start. You see, she knew of the plot against her sister. She had been approached by the man behind it all, who had visited her through the hole in the back fence. He was her very own grand-nephew. He made her an offer of nothing less than the crown itself! But our lady is tried and true, and she absolutely declined. The intruder tried to convince her to join his plot. He coerced her, threatened her, appealed to her patriotism; but as he did not hurt her, she knew he needed her alive. Then she realized the plot was very real, and she feared her secret would get out.

'It was then, with the aid of someone

on the household staff, that she had herself secreted in this room to ride out the plot and hide from the plotters, believing that if they could not find her, they could not force her to join them. She knew that her actions would stop them from acting against her sister, the queen. For almost a week, she was made comfortable here and was even brought her meals — you can see a few miniscule food crumbs upon the floor near the steps. I am afraid that her accomplice was a bit unsteady with the food dishes. If you look more closely, you might notice something else even more important — traces of pepper dust spread along the floor at the wall that stymied the police dog.'

Holmes suddenly bowed down and ran his forefinger across the floor where the wall had been before the secret door had been opened. Then he brought the tip of his finger up to his nose, took a whiff, nodded, and then offered the doctor a sniff.

'Pepper, certainly — but so light as to be almost indistinct.'

'Yes, only a slight trace; but it was enough to throw off Mr. Mac's police dog's sensitive olfactory senses, though not strong enough for any human to notice, nor to overly distress the dog's keen sense of smell and thus give the game away. It was quite well done, and done by a person with excellent knowledge of the canine olfactory senses.'

'You mean Lady Anne?'

'Precisely. Now, where were we? Oh yes. So the lack of dust upon the floor covered up the fact to Mr. Mac and the police that anyone ever came down here. Lady Westcott had feared just such a plot since she had moved back to London from Germany with her husband 20 years ago, and she was prepared for this situation. She was brave — she expected to be murdered in her own bed; killed as was her little dog, Ruby. She would have even welcomed such an outcome, but her life was never in danger. For you see, she was much too valuable alive, and essential to the success of this plot.'

'Oh my! What am I do?' An elderly woman's high-pitched voice suddenly broke into the thoughts of the doctor and the detective now that she had regained consciousness. Watson stood by Lady Westcott's side and comforted her.

'I am a doctor, madam. You are fine now,' Watson stated softly, with well-practiced reassurance.

'You are safe now, Lady Westcott; we are with the police, and no harm shall come to you,' Holmes stated firmly.

'And my little sister, Vicky? Is the queen safe?'

'She is under Special Branch protection, and the plotters have been apprehended. The queen is safe, Lady Anne,' Holmes said softly.

'Thank God!'

'Yes, thank God!' Watson repeated, but at the same time he was also thinking, *And thank Sherlock Holmes!*

'Ach, what is this?' Inspector Alec MacDonald's thick Aberdeen accent rang loudly throughout the basement as he came down the stairs and saw Lady Westcott and the secret room. To say that he was surprised was a vast understatement. He had searched the basement assiduously without any hint of this secret room. Behind him were Gerald the butler and Maria the maid, whom he ushered forward. 'What is going on here, Mr. Holmes? So you have found her!'

'Lady Westcott is alive and well. She has been in hiding, not abducted. However, she was most certainly aided by someone on her household staff in this bit of secrecy,' Holmes stated simply.

MacDonald looked askance at Gerald the butler. 'You knew! You knew and you did not tell me!'

'No, sir, I did not know!' Gerald replied indignantly as a range of emotions overcame him. Suddenly he ran to the bed and held Lady Westcott in his arms, tears of joy running down his face as he mumbled, 'My love! My sweet love! You are returned to us. I thought you were dead or taken captive. Why did you not confide in me? Why keep me in the dark?'

'Oh, my sweet Gerald, please forgive me,' Lady Westcott said in sincere regard through a stream of tears. 'I could not tell you the truth of this matter, as it would only have ensnared you in this vile web of mine. I did it for your protection, my love; please understand that. Next to my sweet sister Victoria and my dearly deceased Simon, you are the light of my life, and I would not see you placed in any danger. Can you ever forgive me?'

'Of course I forgive you, my love,' Gerald said as the two kissed, now enwrapped in each other's arms.

'Well, Mr. Holmes?' MacDonald prompted.

Sherlock Holmes now looked squarely at the maid, Maria. She stepped forward nervously. 'I only did as my mistress commanded.'

'Be kind to my Maria, gentlemen,' said Lady Westcott. 'She only did my bidding, and she kept me well and fed and safe all these many days. God bless her! She is a good girl and loyal to a fault. Thank you, Maria.'

Maria blushed and gave a furtive smile.

'Well, then, there you have it, Mr. Mac,' Holmes said with a smile. 'All tied up neatly, and only the need of a pretty ribbon to top it off. I am sure you can explain in your report to your superiors — and the Home Office. The PM is especially interested in the outcome of this situation, as you might well imagine.'

'I see, Mr. Holmes,' MacDonald replied with some surprise. 'So you'll be taking no credit?'

'None at all, my friend. As far as the world shall know, it was you who solved the Lady Westcott disappearance — quite a feather in your cap, I daresay. However, do not be too precise about the details in any report you make upon this case, and make no mention of my name, or of the fine lady's true relationship to our good queen. I think this may well become a career-maker for you, Mr. Mac, and no one deserves it more.'

'Why, thank you, Mr. Holmes.'

'Think nothing of it. I always recognize talent when I see it.'

'Aye, and I recognize genius when I see it, Mr. Holmes.'

'*Touché*, Mr. Mac!'

'But tell me, how did you unravel this plot and discover the plotters?'

'Just a matter of the right inquiries I made about two newly arrived Russian gentlemen known for their deadly work:

Rostoff and Rutin. My brother Mycroft and his people were on their track since they arrived here of course, but they could not figure out what their game was. So he allowed them to run free — giving them enough rope to hang themselves, so to speak. Their apparently free movement led to the aspects of this case that we now know, from the murder of the little dog Ruby to the secret of Lady Westcott's whereabouts. The German ambassador has also been 'asked' to leave the country and return to Berlin. He has already been sent back home.'

'I still miss my darling Ruby, Inspector MacDonald.'

The big Scot allowed a smile. 'Your little dog was very brave, ma'am.'

'Lady Westcott,' Holmes added in a softer tone, 'I think you should know that one of the key pieces of evidence in identifying the master behind this plot was the bloody teeth marks deeply inflicted upon the German ambassador's arm by your little dog.'

'My grand-nephew, a truly brutal fellow. And my poor Ruby, gone.' Lady

Westcott shed a tear as Gerald comforted her. 'Thank you, Mr. Holmes, for all your help, and you as well, Inspector Mac-Donald.'

Mr. Mac nodded and smiled.

Holmes stated, 'You are most welcome, Lady Anne. Well, then, I believe we have done all that needs to be done here, eh, Watson?'

'Ah, well, certainly, I imagine,' the good doctor replied, a bit flustered by the sudden change in Holmes's demeanor and his seeming rush to leave so quickly.

'Then let us be off! Lady Westcott, we bid you a fond *adieu;* and Mr. Mac — until we meet again!'

'Until we meet again, Mr. Holmes,' Inspector Alec MacDonald said. The usually dour Scotsman offered a broad smile and a wink of the eye.

Sherlock Holmes gave Mr. Mac a quick wink in return, and then he was gone.

12

Baker Street Once Again

'That was a potentially catastrophic situation, Holmes,' Doctor Watson told his detective friend once they were back at their Baker Street digs, each of them lighting up their favorite pipes. Soon pungent swirls of aromatic smoke were drifting throughout their sitting room. Holmes had been contemplative, but suddenly turned talkative.

'Watson, that vile plot could have brought down the monarchy and perhaps even the empire but for Mr. Mac, a feisty old woman, and a little dog that liked to bark at strangers.'

'Yes, I am very much relieved. But it was most complicated, and the German ambassador — that was a dangerous scheme,' Watson noted with a deep sigh. 'Such plotting and machinations could very well lead to war.'

'Indeed. One key aspect that complicated the case,' Holmes explained carefully, 'was that Lady Anne Saxe-Coburg-Saalfeld is the older sister of Queen Victoria. It seems that Lady Anne never wanted the crown in the first place, and she in fact had refused it adamantly upon numerous occasions before good Queen Vic ever ascended the throne way back in '37. Of course this was all kept hush-hush at the time, so few if any outside the most inner circle of royals even knew Victoria had an older sister back home in Germany who was in direct line to become Queen of England, should she want it.'

'I see; but the fact that she did not want the crown — well, I find that rather inconceivable,' the doctor replied, amazed anyone would turn down the opportunity to become the British monarch. 'She had no desire to become queen? It seems quite unique and inconceivable. Certainly complicated.'

Holmes allowed a brief chuckle. 'Complicated is surely the word for it, old man. However, aside from Lady Anne having no desire for the throne, there was one other quite considerable problem — the young lady who would become the future Lady Anne Westcott is a Catholic. She had converted after meeting her future husband, Lord Simon Westcott, who was also of that faith. The thought of Britain having a queen who was a Catholic — a papist, of all things — would have been unthinkable at the time, causing massive complications for the monarchy and the nation. Even today, in our more enlightened times, it would cause much political consternation. Thankfully, Lady Anne made the situation quite tenable by expressing no desire at all for the throne and seeking to live a quiet and most private life. For you see, she knew that her younger sister, little Vicky, would not make a good queen — she knew she would make a great queen. And she was quite correct.'

'Yes, I see that now. Lady Anne certainly was right about the entire situation. Quite the remarkable woman, I would say, Holmes.'

'Yes, most remarkable. As the years passed, after decades when her presence was almost entirely forgotten and obscured by the passage of time and other events, Berlin had become too dangerous for them; so she moved to London with her husband, took up residence in the new home he had built for her on Abercrombie Road, and lived a quiet private life. However, today in 1890, in the fifty-third year of Queen Victoria's reign, the problem reasserted itself once again when her grand-nephew was appointed the German ambassador.

'Aware of Lady Westcott's royal connection, he worked to take advantage of it. Aside from the familial connection, he sought to appeal to her German patriotism, using every form of leverage to convince her to agree to the plot. She, of course, would have nothing of it. Nevertheless, her grand-nephew worked diligently to coerce her — and yet, while still retaining some loyalty to her homeland, she would not divulge the plot or the plotter. She sought to take care of it herself, in her own way, by going into hiding. The success of the plot would have been devastating for the monarchy. As our American friends are fond of saying, England dodged a rather large and dangerous bullet this time.'

'And what of your friend, Mr. Mac?' Watson asked.

'Yes, indeed, what of him? I wonder about him,' Holmes said in a soft and dreamlike tone, and I knew he was thinking of his young protégé. 'I wonder what he is up to right now!'

'I am sure we will be hearing more from him, Holmes.'

'Yes, you can be assured of that. He is quite the talented fellow.'

Historical Note

While Watson's chronicling of the case at Brilstone Manor with Inspector Alec MacDonald occurred in the late 1880s, it did not appear in *The Strand* magazine until 1914 under the title 'The Valley of Fear', at a time when Holmes allowed Watson to publish the case. However, the case of Lady Anne Westcott that occurred one year later, also with Holmes and Inspector MacDonald playing significant roles, has never been told, until now.

Queen Victoria never did have an older

sister, as far as anyone can prove, nor any sister that anyone knows of, so any cover-up of her existence may well have succeeded, or attest to her desire to remain completely out of the spotlight and her fervent wish never to attain the British crown. Or, more likely, the case of Lady Anne Westcott could well be the result of one very large liberty this author has taken with historical fact in the chronicling of this case. I will leave it up to you, dear reader, to decide. However, *if* Queen Victoria ever did have an older sister, history would surely have turned out quite differently.

At birth, Alexandrina Victoria, later to become Queen Victoria, was a princess of the German state of Saxe-Coburg-Saalfeld. She was fifth in line for the British throne after her father's three elder brothers, all of whom died leaving no surviving legitimate children. The key word here may be 'legitimate'.

Queen Victoria reigned over the United Kingdom for over 63 years, from when she ascended the throne at 18 years of age in 1837, ruling until her death in 1901.

She married her first cousin, Prince Albert of Saxe-Coburg and Gotha in 1840, and they had nine children. Prince Albert died in 1861, but their children would grow up to marry into some of the most powerful royal families of Europe. In fact, at the outbreak of World War I in 1914, most of the leaders of the principal nations involved were closely related by blood to the deceased queen.

The first assassination attempt on Queen Victoria's life was in 1840, while she was pregnant and riding in a carriage with her husband, Prince Albert. Another attempt was made while she was riding in her carriage along The Mall in London in 1842, and two months later yet another attempt was made upon her life. One more assassination attempt was made in 1849. In all these attempts upon her life, either the pistols did not fire, or the bullets missed her entirely. Surely Providence was watching over her. In 1850 she was assaulted with a cane by an ex-army officer, which bruised her forehead.

In fact, these early assassination attempts on the life of the queen in the 1840s caused Robert Peel to form the Metropolitan Police, quartered at Scotland Yard, to protect the city from criminals. Policemen, commonly known as 'peelers' or 'bobbies', got their name from Robert Peel.

Queen Victoria's life and reign over the United Kingdom and its possessions and colonies was long and prosperous, and was a golden era of power and stability for the empire she ruled — and the world in general. It defined what would be called the Victorian Era. In September 2015, Queen Victoria's great-granddaughter, Queen Elizabeth II, became the longest reigning British monarch, outlasting Queen Victoria's reign of 63 years and seven months — but never eclipsing it.

The Case of
The Unseen Assassin

1

Josiah Wilson was the first one. Mr. Wilson was a posh young gentleman on his lunch hour from Lloyd's Bank, where he was a newly employed teller. He had always desired a financial situation, and now being newly graduated from university and with a lovely young fiancée and an impending marriage, he seemed quite the up-and-comer. That assertion was assiduously assured when one realized that his future bride-to-be was the only daughter of the well-known and rather excessively wealthy mill owner, Myron Bloom.

Mr. Bloom was said to be worth half a million, and his darling daughter Judith — the apple of his eye — wanted for nothing. Well, she did want for one thing — young Mr. Wilson, and she was on the way to having the man of her dreams become a part of her life forever, while Mr. Wilson was assured of a rising position at Lloyd's after the marriage and the newfound windfall of his wife's finances — courtesy of her doting father, of course.

So it was with a jaunty gait and a smile upon his face that young Josiah Wilson walked down the wide and luxurious expanse of London's Strand, anticipating a future of brilliant success and connubial bliss. However, in a few moments Josiah Wilson was experiencing the shock of his young life.

The strange man approached Wilson rather forcefully, as these types usually do, intruding upon his space with a closeness not at all appreciated. He was a rather down-and-out sad case, and the young man could not help but pity him.

'Got a penny for one what's fought for queen an' country?' the man asked Wilson in a harsh rasping tone; the smell of alcohol was powerful about him, and his ragged clothing left no doubt to anyone about his downward plight.

Wilson looked askance at the fellow, who had seemingly come out from nowhere — or perhaps Wilson had been daydreaming of his new young wife and her overabundance of wealth; but he now saw the man plainly and with some alarm. However, he felt himself to be a decent chap, so felt pity for the poor man. He reached into his vest pocket and withdrew a shilling — quite a large sum to be given to any man; but after all, the ragged fellow had said he was a veteran.

'Here, my good man,' Wilson spoke up, taking a sudden step back from the beggar; for while he did not mind helping him out, he did not want to encourage any close physical contact with the likes of such a person. 'Here, now move off and do right by my generosity.'

The man came in closer, grinning, and touched his fist to his forelock in an act of respect. 'Bless you, sir!'

Wilson allowed a slight grin, feeling good about himself. He was a decent chap, after all.

When the shot was heard, Wilson suddenly felt a hard blow to his chest. It seemed like a very hard punch. Was he having a heart seizure? The blow quite rightly knocked the wind out of him. He gasped in shock, then looked hard into the eyes of the man in front of him as the shilling coin fell from his hand.

The destitute fellow now saw the blood spot spreading in the chest of his young benefactor like a blooming rose, and in dire panic he ran off — though not forgetting to quickly snatch up the coin in a grimy hand before it fell to the ground.

Wilson now also fell to the ground, bloody and bleeding. The fine people walking along the Strand that morning were horrified and shocked by what had just occurred. Women screamed. Couples enjoying a stroll down the luxurious byway ran to cover. They all had heard a gunshot — but whence it had come, no one could say. All everyone wanted to do was just get away to safety. Some later said that a down-and-out beggar had been the one who had shot the young man. Some witnesses were sure of this; others were not. Within a minute Josiah Wilson lay alone and quite dead; and with his death all his many hopes and plans for such a lovely future.

He was just the first.

2

Inspector Lestrade of Scotland Yard was working this case hard. 'We cannot have the quality treated in such a brutal manner right under our very noses here in London. I will not abide it! This Mr. Wilson had everything to live for, and his life was snuffed out by some damnable beggar to whom he refused to give some money. I will not have it! Not the proper thing at all!'

Inspector Alec MacDonald, younger and newer to the force than the venerable Lestrade, did not agree. However, he knew better than to contradict a senior inspector when that man had made up his mind. So he said nothing for the present, but the thoughts were pouring through his mind with frantic energy.

Lestrade looked at the young inspector with a jaundiced eye. Both of them were successful at the Yard, Lestrade over many years with many cases, while MacDonald was younger and showing great promise. Both men had benefited from their collaboration with the well-known consulting detective, Sherlock Holmes.

Lestrade could see that something was bothering the younger man, and that fact was beginning to bother him as well. 'All right now, what is it, MacDonald?' he asked with evident disdain. 'Your trap is shut tight, so you are being overly solicitous. What are you holding back?'

MacDonald cleared his throat nervously and prepared to speak up, masking his thick Aberdeen accent. He was a tall and thin fellow, impeccably dressed in a dark suit topped by a fashionable bowler hat. He had an almost funereal appearance to him. He said simply, 'Aye, sir, I do have some questions.'

'Questions?' Lestrade asked briskly, carefully looking at the young man before him, showing some unabashed annoyance. He eyed this young inspector, thinking he would have made a most excellent funeral director. Perhaps MacDonald had missed his calling. Lestrade saw the man's face showed no sign at all of what he was thinking. He did not like that.

'Well, then, sir, reservations is more like it,' MacDonald explained simply.

'You have reservations? I see. So what are these reservations?' Lestrade asked bluntly, knowing full well that by asking that question, he had now opened up the floodgates to MacDonald's deductive abilities. Why, this cheeky fellow could almost be as difficult as Sherlock Holmes himself — and that was saying a lot.

Lestrade looked carefully once again at the young detective, a man said to be somewhat of a protégé of Sherlock Holmes, of whom Holmes had spoken glowingly, and who was said by him to possess great talent. Well, Lestrade did not see it. No, not at all. Holmes was fond of calling the young inspector 'Mr. Mac' — a familiarity and obvious friendship which rankled Lestrade no end, though of course he would never admit it. After all, he had known Holmes for many more years and had had many more interactions with the fellow than MacDonald, so it should have been he whom Holmes had taken under his wing. Lestrade did not want to consider the thought that he might be somewhat jealous of that situation — the respect and friendship Mr. Holmes showed toward MacDonald, which had never been shown to him. A deep scowl crossed his face at the very thought.

'So? Out with it, MacDonald!'

'Well, sir, with all due respect,' the younger man replied, marshalling his thoughts, 'you say you are looking for a beggar, and that it was this man who shot Josiah Wilson, because Wilson would not give him money?'

'Yes; a logical conclusion, as per the facts of the murder. The beggar — and we will track him down soon, mark my words — was angry that he was being pushed off and that Wilson had refused to give him money, so he shot him. Quite simple. Witnesses all say they saw the beggar approach Wilson and ask him for money. Wilson backed away from him, obviously in fear of what was to come. He must have seen the gun at that point held in the beggar's hand.'

'No gun was found,' MacDonald stated carefully.

'It will be. Obviously the beggar took the murder weapon with him when he fled,' Lestrade replied with a sureness that he felt implicitly. That should have settled things, but he could still see the skeptical look on MacDonald's face. He huffed out in annoyance, 'More? What is it now?'

'Well, sir — and I mean no disrespect by this question — but if the beggar shot Wilson because he would not give him money, why then did he not shoot any of the other men or women that day who were walking along the Strand whom he approached, though each one denied him? He certainly asked more people for money and was refused many times, but he did not shoot anyone else. And where does such a beggar get a gun? The man was said by witnesses to be so destitute he was practically dressed in rags.'

'Well, he was probably a former military man wounded or drummed out of the service and given over to drink,' Lestrade offered with a knowing look. 'It happens with some regularity once the men are released from service. He probably retained his sidearm. The case was open and now it is plainly shut, MacDonald. We find the beggar, we find the killer, and that is that.'

'I think not, sir,' MacDonald stated boldly, standing his ground. He knew that only officers in the army were issued side arms, and while the man might have had a military background — could even have been an officer — none of that meant he had shot Wilson.

Lestrade looked closely at the young inspector, a bit tense now, holding back his frustration at all these annoying questions. He did not appreciate being second-guessed like this, especially by one who was his junior. Why was MacDonald giving him a problem with this case? He spoke up firmly, 'Well, it is over now, and that is that. I am senior to you and this is my case, so that is the way it will go.'

'Yes, that is that, sir, as you say,' MacDonald replied, as was required with a slight nod of his head. Lestrade allowed a slim smile of victory over his junior, but under his breath when Lestrade did not hear him, MacDonald softly whispered, 'That is that — for now.'

3

The second shooting happened in the bright afternoon in the center of busy Piccadilly Circus. The shopping crowds were out and about: well-dressed and successful Londoners out for a stroll to the shops and restaurants to enjoy the day.

Stephen Crafts was among them. He walked briskly down the wide sidewalk in a jovial mood. He was a newly minted MP for the Liberal Party and had just won a contentious election. He had been victorious and was feeling rather pleased about it all just then. Life was indeed good. He was on his way to pick up a new dress for his wife at a nearby shop as a gift when he noted a man approaching him from ahead. He recognized the man instantly, of course. It was none other than Sir Thomas Maxwell, the former Tory MP of his district whom he had beaten in the recent election. Crafts smiled; the election had been a bitter fight. The Liberals had taken the seat from the Conservative Party — the blasted Tories — and now Crafts was in and Maxwell was out. The fact that the former MP was probably quite bitter about the loss seemed evident upon his face as he approached.

'Stephen,' Sir Thomas Maxwell spoke as he stopped in front of his former political adversary, who also had now stopped walking to chat with him.

'Sir Thomas, it is good to see you,' Crafts began in a pleasant tone. After all, the election was done and won. No need to rub in the loss. 'No hard feelings, I hope.'

'No hard feelings? Your party cheated me out of my seat in Parliament and I am to have no hard feelings upon the matter?' Maxwell said sternly. He could be a rather cantankerous individual. 'Some of those voters were not qualified at all. I shall demand a recount.'

'That is within your rights,' Crafts acknowledged in an agreeable tone. 'The election was very close.'

'Indeed it was. Well, I sought you out to tell you man to man, sir.'

'That is good of you to do so,' Crafts replied so agreeably that Maxwell could not repress a slim smile.

'Then we shall see what the future holds,' Maxwell added.

'Indeed,' Crafts said calmly.

'Well, I am surprised to see that you are taking it so well,' Maxwell allowed with a sharp nod of his head.

'No need. If things go your way, I am resolved to that change; but they shall not,' Crafts returned with his own slight grin.

Sir Thomas Maxwell nodded. Well, that certainly seemed fair. He reached out his hand in a gentlemanly gesture, and was about to say some kind words, when a loud report was heard. The sound was sharp and echoed through the canyon of buildings all around them. Everyone in the area looked about them in surprise and shock. Maxwell looked behind him nervously — for it sounded as if there had been a gunshot which had come from that direction. When Sir Thomas Maxwell turned back to speak to Stephen Crafts upon the matter, he was shocked to find the man laying upon the ground bleeding profusely from a wound in his chest.

'My God! Quick! Someone! We need a doctor here straight away!' Maxwell cried out as he knelt down in an attempt to staunch the flow of blood from the wounded man. They were not friends — in fact they were mortal political enemies — but they were, after all, proper British gentlemen. One always strove to help a fellow man in need. It was the only proper British thing to do, after all.

The crowd saw the blood and screamed in panic and ran for shelter. Soon bobby whistles were heard shrieking through the chaos, and then a brace of constables was upon the scene. They looked down upon Stephen Crafts with hopeless resignation — they had seen this type of thing many times before.

Sir Thomas Maxwell shouted, 'Help him! He is bleeding to death!'

'Sir,' the senior constable spoke up, shaking his head, 'I'm afraid he's already gone.'

4

'Lestrade?' Inspector Alec MacDonald asked the senior inspector, knowing he had to be careful questioning his superior in such a manner. 'So what do you make of this Crafts murder? Out in Piccadilly in broad daylight — and he was a newly minted Liberal MP.'

'Yes, and as such the Yard and Sir Charles Maine, our superior, have put it on a high level to be solved quickly. I am hard upon the case.'

'So what do you make of it?'

Lestrade thought it over before answering. Was this another trap set by the wily MacDonald? Lestrade had, of course, already questioned the former Tory MP, Sir Thomas Maxwell, who had been present at the scene of the murder. Lestrade immediately ruled out Maxwell, as such a gentleman was unthinkable as the killer. He also had questioned both men's wives about the election, and the party leaders, including another Liberal Party member named Jones who had challenged Crafts and lost to him in a bitter fight. Here Lestrade found some enmity that could surely be a motive for murder. Jones owned a rifle like the one used to kill Crafts, and it had been shown to have been fired recently. Jones had told Lestrade that it had been fired because he had recently gone out hunting, but when asked to produce witnesses to that statement, he could not do so; he said he had gone hunting alone.

Lestrade shook his head, sneering at what he considered a thinly disguised lie. He looked at MacDonald. 'I think I have our killer. No man goes hunting alone. It is a group social activity, so his alibi was easily transparent to me. In fact, I believe Jones was jealous as he had not been given the party nod to run. He seemed to resent Crafts bitterly as a result.'

MacDonald listened without comment and showed no sign of what he was thinking.

Lestrade continued with a knowing grin. 'Yes, I believe it was Jones who did the deed. Revenge, jealousy, treachery — who can say? He owns a rifle and is a hunter. The rifle has recently been fired and he has no firm alibi. I mean, gone out hunting alone? That is shaky. In fact, it is unheard of! No one goes out hunting alone. Crafts was killed at a distance with just such a rifle. The fact that Jones owns the same type of rifle as the bullet found in Crafts' body tells me all I need to know. His gun had been fired recently, no doubt at the murdered man. I am sure I have our culprit.'

MacDonald shook his head in surprise and frustration. He did not agree at all. However, this was getting to be a delicate situation, and he could now see very well why Sherlock Holmes had such disdain for Lestrade. The man was a bulldog for sure; once on the scent he would never give up the chase until he closed the case — and this was to his credit — but too often he was set on the *wrong* scent.

'Jones did not do it!' MacDonald pointed out plainly.

'Not do it? Then who the hell did?'

'I do not know.'

'Hah, now that is so typical. More conjecture and deductive logic like our friend Mr. Holmes is fond of using? Well, MacDonald, it is not needed here now. I have just closed two important murder cases,' Lestrade said with some satisfaction, though he saw the dire look on the other man's face and was troubled by it. 'Now what?'

'I cannot believe you would say that,' MacDonald stated.

'Oh yes, and I say it with firm conviction. I'll tell you something else: I have also found the beggar, and he will soon be placed in the dock for the murder of Josiah Wilson. So you see, I have things well in hand,' Lestrade told his junior triumphantly.

'Of course the beggar denies the murder?'

'Of course, but that is to be expected,' Lestrade replied with a shrug.

MacDonald pursed his lips in exasperation. There seemed nowhere else to go with this, except perhaps — 'So I presume the murder weapon was found on the beggar?'

'No,' Lestrade replied slowly, 'but it is of little consequence. The man did the deed plain as day. We have many witnesses. He hid the gun, of course. We may find it, or we may not, but I am sure we have our man. Case closed.'

MacDonald was horrified by Lestrade's cavalier attitude concerning such a life and death situation, but he knew better than to engage in battle with a senior inspector. 'And now this Crafts murder — an MP, no less. It is an important case, and quite a feather in your cap to solve it so quickly.'

Lestrade preened at the compliment. Now MacDonald was talking sense. 'It is, and I put it all down to good dogged detective work.'

'Of that I am sure,' MacDonald replied softly, but his tone of irony and cynicism was lost upon Lestrade.

5

'Well, Holmes, why so glum this morning?' Doctor John Watson asked his friend, the consulting detective, Sherlock Holmes. It was an early spring morning in 1894, and there had been a lull in cases. The two men were ensconced comfortably in their sitting room at 221B Baker Street. Holmes was smoking furiously upon one of his favorite pipes while Watson was reading one of the daily newspapers.

Sherlock Holmes did not reply to the doctor's question. Watson continued offhandedly, 'Ah, what's this? I see Lestrade has made an arrest on the Josiah Wilson murder case. Some beggar or such, it appears, was the culprit.'

'I am aware of it, Watson,' Holmes replied rather coldly.

'Quite a feather in Lestrade's cap, I should say; and he did it all on his own this time and without any help from you. Bravo for him!'

'Bravo, indeed.'

'Why so glum, Holmes? By all accounts it was a rather simple open-and-shut case — nothing up to your requirements featuring anything of unique interest. Do not be jealous of his little victory; it does not suit you, my friend.'

'Jealous? Watson, read between the lines and you will see that not all makes sense in this case. I believe Lestrade has made a grievous error. I have contacted him upon this very matter, and on one other recent murder in the news — the killing of the MP in Piccadilly — but he refuses to listen to me on either case.'

'I'm afraid I don't understand,' Watson said, putting down his paper and looking over at his friend carefully. 'Has some mistake been made?'

'Indeed it has! In fact, major mistakes have been made!' Holmes stated sharply. He was tense, visibly upset at the prospect. 'I will give him this: Lestrade has a zeal for closing cases — but unfortunately he closes them whether he is right or wrong!'

'Well then, if what you say is true, a

terrible injustice has been done. It must be corrected.'

'Lestrade has precipitated not one, but two injustices, Watson! The beggar did not kill Wilson. The Liberal member Jones did not kill the MP Crafts. However, there is much more to this than first meets the eye, and I will endeavor to find it out whether Lestrade calls me in on it or not.'

'I see. I naturally agree with you, but what do you mean there is more to this? You have already told me that the two men accused by the police are innocent. Then what else is there?' Watson asked, showing his evident concern.

'What else — ? Yes, that is the question, my friend. I have suspicions; I see a pattern, and I am sure that there is a connection between these two murders. I have told Lestrade this and he refuses to listen. I have also made Mr. Mac aware of my thoughts on the matter, but he does not have the authority to pursue these two cases as he would like to. Lestrade is senior. He is in control.'

'Well, what else can there be to this?'

Watson asked curiously.

'I do not know that yet. You know my methods; I never theorize before I have all the facts in hand. But I do have one or two ideas based on the facts that we do have. These we can investigate now on our own, if the official police will not do so,' Holmes stated firmly.

'What do you want me to do, Holmes?' Watson asked with growing excitement. He was glad to see the prospect of some action on a new case. 'You know all you need to do is ask and I will do anything I can to help you.'

'Good man, Watson! I knew I could count on you. I believe that these two murders — Wilson and Crafts — are indeed connected somehow. We must find that connection.'

'How do we do that?'

'We look deeper into Wilson and Crafts.'

'What can I do to help?' Watson asked, putting down his newspaper.

Holmes walked over to Watson and picked up the newspaper. 'This is what you shall do, my friend. You are to check the daily papers for all murders in and around London for the last ... let us begin by going back three months. See what you can find and make notes. You will have to go to the newspaper offices and delve into their morgues of back issues. I can give you the names of men there who will allow you access on my behalf.'

'That's it?'

'For now. We are trying to establish a connection. What kind of connection, I don't know as yet.'

'All right, Holmes.'

'There is something else.'

'Yes?'

'In your search of the London papers, be alert to any reports of murders on foreign shores — specifically America or Europe, where it has been reported that there has been a string of murders of men that have gone unsolved, or where much controversy surrounds such crimes.'

'I'm afraid I don't understand, Holmes,' Watson replied, a bit overwhelmed by the length and depth of the request, 'but I shall do all you say.'

'Good man, Watson! With any luck, we

will discover something that puts this all into perspective.'

'I certainly hope so.'

6

'Not another one,' Scotland Yard Inspector Alec MacDonald had said, allowing his frustration to show. He had been sent out by his superior, Sir Charles Maine, to investigate a recent shooting in the Strand of another well-to-do gentleman. Lestrade was busy, his hands full with his two earlier cases, so this one had fallen into MacDonald's lap. He was eager to get to it and become involved.

He reached the Strand soon enough. The area was a district of better shops and some finer homes for the upper classes. It was the roaming grounds of high-hat toffs and lovely ladies; certainly not the kind of place for murder and death.

'Yes, sir, this is it,' the bobby on the scene of the killing stated when the inspector came over to him. MacDonald nodded, happy to see that the murdered man's body had not yet been removed from the pavement, as it was now common practice to await the arrival of an official detective. However, the bobby had tastefully covered the corpse with his long coat and kept back the crowd. This young constable was on the ball.

'Shot in the 'ead, 'e was, sir. Killed instantly, I'd say. That's the third one in as many weeks,' the bobby added in a conspiratorial whisper. 'The papers are making rather a lot of it.'

'Aye,' MacDonald said thoughtfully. It was the third murdered man in as many weeks, and it was becoming a serious problem. While Lestrade had told the press that all was well in hand, the press did not believe him, perhaps just on general principle or past history. In any case, news of the killings was being reported more sensationally in the tabloids, and that news was beginning to unnerve the public, almost as much as the Ripper murders had done six years previously. However, these seemingly random shootings targeted the quality and the upper classes, and that made it much more difficult for the public to deal with. These were not street people or prostitutes, but gentlemen of consequence or of some higher expectation. One had even been a rising young MP!

Naturally, the papers were all over the story by now and they had even dubbed the mysterious killer 'The Unseen Assassin' because he apparently chose his victims from those men peacefully walking up and down some of the most prestigious and glamorous avenues and boulevards of London, though the killer had never been seen by any witnesses. He was like a shadow who disappeared after his deadly deed was done.

'The Unseen Assassin has struck again, Inspector,' the young bobby said with a twinge of fear in his voice. He looked about him furtively as if he himself might be another target. He then looked over at the inspector for guidance.

MacDonald only nodded and looked closely at the face of the dead man lying upon the ground at his feet. The bullet hole was in the man's head, which seemed to indicate a small-caliber weapon, some discreet handgun such as a woman might use. That meant the dead man had been done in up close and personal. Or, just perhaps, the weapon could have been a small-caliber rifle, and the killing shot taken from far away — but that would mean a marksman of considerable skill and ability; a hunter, or a military man.

MacDonald looked down at the dead man once more. He was a well-dressed man of business, in his middle years, well-off, and rather distinguished-looking. He wondered if he would have anything in common with the previously murdered men, aside from the obvious. He would have to check all connections — friends, family, work. Were they members of the same clubs? All these men were successful, but that was not enough of a connection; that was just the starting place. There had to be more. Probably much more!

'There *has* to be a link,' MacDonald whispered to himself.

'Eh, sir, what's that you said?' the bobby asked curiously.

'Nothing. I was just saying that there has to be some link between this man and the two earlier men who were murdered.

There's something I'm missing.'

'Well they're all well-off toffs, for sure,' the bobby offered, stating the obvious.

MacDonald nodded his head. Yes, that was true. Now what else? There had to be more. He would have to dig much deeper.

And he did. The next few days, Inspector MacDonald spent every waking hour on this third murder. The man's name was Simon Simonson, another banker — this time not some lowly clerk like Wilson, but one of the directors of the august First London Bank. The killer seemed to be moving up in the world of his targets. MacDonald's theory, augmented by Holmes's note to him upon the matter a week before, had been that the murders of Wilson, Crafts, and now Simonson were from the onset all connected in some way.

Lestrade and his superiors at the Yard did not believe this theory at all, even when MacDonald noted the fact that the great Sherlock Holmes supported it. They had their killers, and they did not need the sensational and terrifying story of another Ripper-type killer running loose in London to upset the public. Lestrade had already arrested men for the first two murders. MacDonald feared for the poor unfortunates, as well as any new suspect Lestrade would soon accuse of Simonson's murder — the supposed third killer. Perhaps some foreigner, or some poor fellow on the skids. The only thing MacDonald knew was that Lestrade would be wrong about his suspect.

MacDonald did not believe the panic headlines, and was sure that while the killings were devious and horrific, they did not rise to the level of anything to compare with the Ripper killings. The Ripper murder victims had all been female prostitutes — women from the lowest end of the social scale — and each one had been horribly mutilated. These three murders were all males, and successful men at that. The three men had each been neatly shot with one bullet, and each of these men had had much to live for. It was perplexing. There had to be some kind of conspiracy or master plan — some connection he was not seeing. Finding that connection was the difficult part of solving these three murders. It was seemingly impossible, but MacDonald was convinced that connection did exist.

Inspector MacDonald looked everywhere, searched all localities, sought out and talked to all the witnesses of all three murders. He spoke to anyone connected with the murdered men. He was taking a chance by expanding his investigation so wide and inserting himself into Lestrade's cases, but he knew he had to do more background work there to find any connection between Lestrade's two murders and his own case. He found nothing, however. Other than the obvious fact that all three murdered men had been successful to varying degrees, there seemed to be no connection at all. They did not know each other. They did not even know the same people.

MacDonald thought of Sherlock Holmes, and considered bringing him the problem and seeking his advice. The man was already somewhat interested, as evidenced by his note to MacDonald telling him he believed the first two cases were connected. Mac-Donald had not seen the consulting detective in almost four years, since the Lady Anne Westcott case had been cleaned up. Now that had been a loopy but very dangerous situation. MacDonald felt that this one was in that same complex category — different for certain, of course, but just as serious and just as deadly.

He decided that he would drop by Baker Street and visit his old friends Sherlock Holmes and Doctor Watson. It would be good to see them again, whether they were able to help him with this case or not.

7

The building at 221 Baker Street was much as MacDonald remembered it. This section of central London seemed to always remain the same, and he liked that arrangement just fine. There was a comforting feeling of warmth and reassurance even as his footsteps took him closer to the building.

'I say, Holmes,' Watson said to his companion softly from his place where he was looking out the front window. 'You were right as rain, old man. I see him coming here now.'

'Mr. Mac?'

'The very same.'

'Good.' Holmes smiled, looking over at Watson. 'You did your work for me well. You discovered some interesting facts — a couple that seemingly slipped through the cracks. The window cleaner's death I find of particular interest.'

'They say it was an accident. You think

he was murdered?'

'We do not yet possess all the facts, so we shall see what we find there.'

'But the man is dead, Holmes. His head was smashed in the fall, and there was no bullet wound found anywhere else upon the body.'

'Correct, unless he had been shot in the head.'

'I see.' The doctor nodded, digesting that bit of data. 'And then there was the woman in the park.'

'Yes; a wound in the leg, you told me. She said she had been shot.' Holmes walked back and forth in the small open area of their sitting room. 'I believe that woman, Mrs. Spicer, had been the victim of a bullet wound by our man — but of a ricocheted bullet. It seems our assassin missed his target that day, or she interfered with the shot. In any case, he seems to be a very able shot, perhaps even a marksman, but not perfect. Nothing ever is. In fact, the more I think about it, I believe the woman got in the way of his shot. I am certain he was not aiming at her.'

'So now we have at least five attempts that we know of,' Watson said, counting on his fingers. 'Mrs. Spicer was the first, which was a miss.'

'Yes, but she was not the target,' Holmes interrupted.

'Quite right,' Watson agreed with a firm nod of his head. 'Next there was the window cleaner, then Josiah Wilson, then Crafts; and finally the most recent was this banker, Simonson — but no one has been brought to book for that one yet.'

'And no one shall be. Not for a while, at least. I am sure this is the case which our Mr. Mac has been given — just as I am sure that Lestrade 'cleared up' the Wilson and Crafts murders so quickly, in his own way of course, by arresting the wrong men. Innocent men.'

'My God, Holmes! That is a truly terrible thought. They will be placed in the dock and could get the noose for these crimes. If they are indeed innocent . . . '

'They *are* innocent. That is why I had you do some digging at the newspaper morgues. I assume Cruthers and Tiny were helpful?'

'Yes, but where do you ever meet such people? They are like troglodytes, inhabiting a section of sub-basement buildings I had never known existed here in London.'

'Yes; they are unique creatures in their own way, but very useful and knowledgeable. Like the hospital morgue you are more familiar with, newspaper morgues are the places where old stories go to die — but they never truly die, Watson. The record rooms contain all the hidden facts. Have you ever heard of the Frenchman, Huret?'

'I can't say that I have.'

'Yes, you missed that one, but it is not your fault. Then have you ever heard of the Boulevard Assassin of Paris?'

'Yes, now that you mention him I do remember it! It had been all the rage on the continent at the time, and even written about somewhat in the papers here — a year or two ago I think. But the French authorities arrested him and he was convicted, I remember reading. So that was Huret? I think I read that the killer was hung for his crimes in Paris, was he not?'

'Huret was indeed executed, but it was by madame guillotine. However, whether he was the actual Boulevard Assassin of Paris appears to be quite another matter now.'

'Really? Are you sure? Why, that is terrible, Holmes!'

'What is terrible is that it is taking our friend Mr. Mac so much time to decide to come here to seek our help in this matter. He surely should have been up here by now,' Holmes said, allowing his impatience to show.

'Well, he has his pride, you know.'

'We all have our pride, Watson. However, the paramount focus should be on solving the case properly — and damn all pride!'

'You are correct, as usual.'

'Hah!' Holmes blurted in a cynical tone. 'You know last week I put my theory on this case to Lestrade, telling him that the Wilson and Crafts murders were connected; but he said he had his killers in hand and did not need my help, thank you very much.'

'The scoundrel!'

'I also put it to Mr. Mac, and with him my theory received a far more serious hearing — but of course he was not on the case then.'

'Well, he is now, Holmes.'

'Yes, he is, Watson! And that means *we* are as well!'

At that moment there was a knock to the downstairs door.

'That will be Mr. Mac. He is finally here. Now we begin!' Holmes stated, rubbing his hands together in eager anticipation.

8

'Mr. Holmes, Doctor, it is good to see you both again after so long,' Inspector Alec MacDonald said briskly as he walked into the sitting room of 221B and warmly shook hands with his old friends and comrades in arms, so to speak, once again. The room appeared to him much as it had four years earlier. It seemed little changed here in the world of Mr. Holmes and Doctor Watson: the furniture, the paintings, the fireplace, with books and papers scattered all around as they had always been — what he considered to be an organized mess — was all strangely comforting to the Scotland Yard inspector.

'And I you, Mr. Mac,' Holmes replied in a friendly manner, obviously happy to see the talented young Scotland Yard detective once again. When Mr. Mac came to him with a case, it always promised to be something unique and outré, possessing those qualities that so stimulated Holmes's deductive abilities. Watson felt that his friend actually lived for such challenges.

'So where do we begin, Mr. Holmes?'

'You tell us, Mr. Mac. We are here for you, and now entirely at your disposal.'

'Thank you,' MacDonald said with genuine respect. He marshaled his thoughts. 'Well, to be frank, Lestrade has it all wrong, first of all.'

'Of course,' Holmes agreed with a wry nod and a dismissive wave of his hand. 'Let us stipulate that. The two men, the beggar and Jones, are innocent, and we shall prove that in due course, rest assured. But before that is done, we must find the actual killer.'

'Yes,' MacDonald agreed. 'And that is the problem.'

'So you have no doubt that these three murders are connected?'

'No, none.'

'I agree,' Sherlock Holmes said with a nod, happy to see that the inspector was in agreement with him. 'Watson and I have been doing a bit of digging on our own.'

'You have?'

'Yes, and we have discovered that Josiah Wilson was not the first man killed by this so-called Unseen Assassin, as the press have rather sensationally dubbed him.'

'Yes, the Unseen Assassin is what the rags of the popular press are now calling him. It is a travesty; a scheme to sell papers. They are even comparing his killings to the Ripper murders.'

'Well, they may not be far off on that score. This is at least as serious,' Holmes offered in a dry tone. 'In any case, your Mr. Wilson was not the first murder, and I am sure there will be more to come unless this man is stopped soon.'

'I agree,' MacDonald said with a nod of his head, for he had already figured that out on his own. The killer was of that violent obsessive type who would continue his deadly deeds until he was stopped. 'But what do you mean that Wilson was not the first murder?'

'I will get to that in due course. Have you ever heard of Huret, the Boulevard Assassin of Paris?' Holmes asked the inspector.

MacDonald thought for a moment. 'Some sensational case a year or two back in France. I recall it barely made the papers here.'

'Surely not reported in any serious detail, unfortunately. Nevertheless, it is most interesting. Huret was an anarchist eventually arrested and convicted of shooting random people in the better sections of Paris. He was one of the many socialist radicals and violent anarchists that have been causing havoc in Paris lately. Huret was convicted and executed. The killings then stopped. Those are the facts.'

'Then what does he have to do with the killings here in London, Mr. Holmes? Huret is dead. Do you suspect another anarchist?'

'I am not sure yet, Mr. Mac. We have some work to do first. I have sent a telegram to Inspector Franco of La Surete Nationale in Paris, and am eagerly anticipating his reply. In the meantime, would you like to accompany Watson and myself on a visit to the Amalgamated Insurance Building?'

Mr. Mac looked a bit bewildered by the request. He grinned and said, 'I am not in need of any insurance at this time, Mr. Holmes.'

Sherlock Holmes allowed a slight smile.

Watson quickly jumped into the breach to explain. 'That is the building where the window cleaner worked. Holmes believes he was our killer's first victim.'

Mr. Mac nodded. 'Aye, I see. Then yes, Mr. Holmes, I would be glad to accompany you, for now it appears that I am at *your* service.'

'Only for a short time; but who knows what we will discover.'

9

The building that housed Amalgamated Insurance Ltd. was a prestigious eight-story edifice in central London's business district that was well suited to an old and well-respected firm. It contained many offices, and hence many windows that needed washing due to the ever-present soot and smog in the London air; hence a staff of four men was employed full-time to clean them on a weekly basis. They were professionals at their job and had been doing it for many years.

Sherlock Holmes, Doctor Watson and Inspector MacDonald were brought by the managing director to the office of the building maintenance manager, who was to take care of their needs.

'Investigating old Barney's death, are you?' Mr. Thomson asked the trio. He was surprised that the coppers were here for this. It was common knowledge that Barney had slipped and fallen to his death. A tragic bit of work that, but the profession was fraught with danger, especially from sudden gusts of wind when a man was outside on a ledge.

'Yes we are,' MacDonald replied firmly.

'Well I don't see why. Barney got careless and just fell. It happens. A bloke goes out on the ledge, fails to hook his safety line, or gets dizzy — some of the boys are known to visit the pubs the night before, if you know what I mean. I'm sure some even take a few nips while working out on the ledge, though it is most definitely frowned upon. However, it happens and cannot be helped.'

'Drinking while performing that line of work is extremely dangerous,' Watson chided, shocked by the man's casual words.

'Was Barney drunk that morning?' Holmes asked Thomson.

'No, he was not.'

'How do you know?' MacDonald asked quickly.

'Old Barney was a teetotaler. Never a drop of alcohol passed his lips since I knew him,' Thomson replied with a confident nod of his head.

'Interesting,' Holmes said. 'Mr. Thomson, can you take us to the exact window that Barney was washing when he fell to his death?'

'Yes; follow me up to the eighth floor, Accounting Section. I know just the window.' He led the trio to one of the new Otis elevators, which took them up to the eighth floor. The ride in the wooden car proved to be rather slow and jerky, and all four men were relieved when it was over.

Once the elevator stopped on the eighth floor and the doors were opened, Thomson said in a grumpy tone, 'This is a new-fangled bloody Yank contraption. Sometimes it gets stuck. I always say a little prayer when I take it up or down, but it surely beats the hell out of walking up and down all those bloody steps. Now just follow me, gentlemen.'

Holmes and his companions were led to a corner office in an empty part of the floor. There was no occupant.

'That window right there, good sirs. Barney was just coming back in from washing it, I imagine, when he lost his grip and fell,' Thomson offered, pointing to the window in question.

'Did anyone see him fall, or did he call out?' Holmes asked.

Mr. Thomson shook his head. 'No; the room here was temporarily empty. Barney must have lost his balance; he did break the window with his fall. It has since been replaced. Other than that, there's nothing more to say on the matter. Barney was a good lad; we all miss him.'

'Thank you,' Holmes said, dismissing the man as his eyes scanned the room more carefully. There were four large glass windows in the office. They were closed, but the shades were raised to let the sunshine into the room. It was quite bright.

'Holmes, the window was broken — that means Barney fell *into* the room,' Watson said. 'So how did he fall *back* and down to the ground? It makes no sense to me.'

'An interesting observation, my dear fellow.'

'Perhaps if the man lost his balance, he could have fallen inward toward the window, broken the glass, and then lost his balance again and fallen backwards and down to the ground,' observed MacDonald.

'That is possible, Mr. Mac, but you are both missing the main question here. That question is this: was Barney's death a murder that is connected to these later murders?'

'I do not think so now,' Watson mused.

'How can we tell?' MacDonald asked Holmes.

Sherlock Holmes looked around the room carefully but did not reply.

Watson continued, 'I examined the window cleaner's body. It was still at the morgue, unclaimed, when I went there yesterday; it appears old Barney had no family. When I examined the corpse, I could find no bullet holes. He was not shot as far as I could tell.'

'And what of the man's head, Watson?'

'Well, Holmes, of course I could not make out much from what was left of that, as there was little left at all. The man's fall had obliterated his skull.'

'So what then if he was shot in the

head?' Holmes asked the doctor.

'Well, if he had been shot in the head, then there would be no evidence of that on the corpse, I am afraid.'

Holmes nodded, showing a hint of satisfaction. 'Then since that avenue is closed to us, we shall just have to find another way.'

'How do we do that, Mr. Holmes?' MacDonald asked, somewhat surprised. 'If the window cleaner had been shot in the head, his fall destroyed any evidence of that fact upon the body. We are back to where we started.'

'Well, we shall see, but I find it very bright in here. The sun is hurting my eyes. Inspector, would you mind very much pulling down that shade there?'

'This one?'

'Yes, that one.'

MacDonald shrugged and then did as he was asked. The shade that Holmes had indicated was pulled down to cover the window, and the room grew slightly darker as the sun was blocked — except for one tiny round hole in the shade that let through the sun in a long, bright pinpoint ray of sunshine.

'Aye, I see it now!' MacDonald gasped in disbelief.

'A bullet hole in the shade!' Watson blurted in surprise.

'Precisely, Watson. And I believe, Mr. Mac, that if you follow that ray of light and search the molding on the opposite wall that it points to, you will find embedded there the slug from the bullet our Unseen Assassin used to kill Barney the window cleaner.'

Inspector MacDonald followed the path of the slim ray of sunlight, examined the part of the wall Holmes had indicated, and soon found the slug. He used a penknife to dig it out of the wall. 'Here it is, Mr. Holmes, just as you said!'

10

The trio were now back at Baker Street digesting what they had learned from their morning outing.

'Aye, I am raging with anger now,' MacDonald stated in a blistering tone, allowing full vent to his thick Aberdeen accent. 'I missed two earlier attempts by this assassin; for as you say, Mr. Holmes, the wounded woman in the park, Mrs. Spicer, must have been the first — a miss for our killer. Then that made poor Barney the first kill, as far as we have discovered. So we have four murders so far, at least, that we know of.'

'Yes, they are all connected, done by the same man, with the same rifle,' Holmes answered, thinking it all through.

'But why, Holmes? What is the reason?' Watson asked, as the mystery seemed to only be growing deeper.

'Aye, Mr. Holmes, I've been trying to figure that out for two weeks since you brought the matter to my attention. I canna see a thing! There seems no connection among these people at all.'

'Yes, the connection is very difficult to determine,' Holmes replied in a low tone. 'At first we could see that these men were all connected, albeit loosely, by their success or class; but Barney the window cleaner may preclude even that theory.'

'Then we are surely up the junction,' MacDonald stated glumly.

'Perhaps our killer is merely moving up to better prey,' Watson suggested.

'Perhaps, for he is certainly hunting his victims. Though just why he is doing so eludes me so far.'

'Then what are we to do?' MacDonald asked, his voice showing the frustration he felt so keenly. 'How can I catch such a killer? How can I determine where and when he will strike next? If I knew that, perhaps I could stop him.' He looked to Holmes for some helpful comment or direction.

Sherlock Holmes only sat down and picked up his pipe and began stuffing it with his favorite tobacco. 'I will need some time to delve into the particular facts of this case — alone.'

Inspector MacDonald glanced over at him curiously, but Holmes ignored him now and was soon surrounded by a growing fog of thick tobacco smoke as he puffed away like a locomotive upon his favorite meerschaum.

MacDonald nodded, recalling Holmes's sometimes aloof manner. 'Well, Doctor, perhaps we should be off. A pint of bitter would do me a world of good right now. Will you join me?'

'Of course,' Watson replied as he put on his coat. He knew that his friend needed some time alone to turn the problem over in that marvelous mind of his in silence, and without interruption or distraction.

'See you later, Holmes,' MacDonald said over his shoulder.

There was no reply from Sherlock Holmes as the two men left the room.

11

It was dark and much later when Watson strolled none too gently or quietly into the rooms of 221B.

'More than a pint or two, I take it,' came the sharp harangue from Sherlock Holmes. The great detective was seated in the same chair he had been in when Watson had left him hours ago, and he seemed to have not moved the position of his body at all since then.

Watson smiled foolishly. 'MacDonald and I got to talking. You know how it is.'

'Indeed. Well, while you and the inspector were chumming it up at the local pub, a telegram came for me from Paris. It is upon the breakfast table; Mrs. Hudson brought it up just before you returned. Would you be so good as to open it up and read it?'

Watson nodded, saw the envelope, opened it and began reading the message. 'It is from Paris, Holmes; from Commandant

Franco of the Surete.'

'Please read it to me, Watson.'

My Dear Monsieur Sherlock Holmes, I am in receipt of your inquiry into the Huret case here in Paris. A most distasteful affair. I can assure you that Huret was convicted and duly executed for the crimes. The body was definitely that of Huret.

'That is all?' Holmes asked anxiously.

'No, there's another section lower down on the letter.'

'And what does that say?'

Watson's face slowly changed to one of growing distress as he began to read:

Monsieur Holmes, as to your other question, I pray that it will not prove to be true. I have endeavored to inquire more deeply, and must tell you now that I believe with great despair that you may be correct in your assertion. Mon Dieu!

Watson put down the letter, fearing that he now realized its import. His face was ashen, and his lips could only whisper the question, 'Correct about what?'

'Watson, sometimes it is not so pleasant to be proven right, I think,' Holmes said with a dark expression.

'What does it mean? What was the second question you asked Commandant Franco?'

'I asked him if there was a possibility they may have executed the wrong man.'

'An innocent man!'

'Yes.'

Watson was horrified. His worst fears upon the matter had been proven true.

12

'I know that such things happen all the time, even here in our good English judicial system, but the thought of any innocent man going to his death in an execution is most upsetting; appalling, really,' Watson said. His energy had left him and he was feeling dejected at the prospect of such an affront to justice.

'Yes, that is true; but the real problem we have now is that because this man Huret was executed for the murders perpetrated by another man, *that* man is still loose — and it appears that he is killing again now here in London.'

'The real killer, here now! They are one and the same?'

'Yes; he began his deadly deeds in Paris, and escaped detection when poor Huret was nabbed for the crimes. It may have been a set-up. In any case, he came here to England — I wonder why? But he laid low for a year or so. That also poses certain questions. However, it may just be that the man's natural homicidal tendencies could not be held in check any longer. He continued to kill. Perhaps he believes that since he was able to get away with his murders the first time, he would get away with them again here in London. I pray not; but with men like Lestrade arresting every innocent man in sight for these murders, I am afraid to say that our next Huret may be in the making, Watson.'

'That is certainly a grim thought. So what are we to do? How can we catch such a mysterious criminal? MacDonald is a good man, but seems to find himself at a loose end.'

'I feel his angst, believe me,' Holmes said carefully. 'And still I ask myself, what is the connection here?'

'Perhaps there is no connection, Holmes,' Watson offered with a shake of his head.

'No, I cannot accept that, my friend. Logic dictates there must be something that ties all these men together, and to their murderer. If we can discover that, I am sure we can find the killer.'

'Well, I for one cannot see it.'

'Neither can I, Watson. But I will give it some more time; it may show itself soon enough. I just pray that we do not have to wait for any more murders to occur before we can obtain the evidence we need. In the meantime, you and I, and Mr. Mac with his men, will question all the principals and witnesses once more and in greater detail. We shall press them hard, and squeeze out of them any neglected fact or unobtrusive detail they may have left out. There surely must be a connection, and I will not rest until I find it.'

13

The next murder was at noon in the middle of the rushing mob and hubbub that moved so quickly through Charing Cross. It was one of the local shopkeepers, an older gentleman who ran one of the bookstores off the Strand. He had been going to a nearby tearoom when he suddenly fell to the ground. Passersby ran over to help the man, who they assumed had fainted or had taken ill. It was only then that his helpers saw the blood pooling in the street from a bullet wound in the old man's neck. Mr. Mathias Snelling, beloved rare bookseller, had died instantly.

Inspector MacDonald was on the scene immediately, and he called for Sherlock Holmes and Doctor Watson to meet him. The three men looked over the body. There was no doubt that Mr. Snelling had been shot, as a bullet wound was unmistakable. This was the first time that

Sherlock Holmes had been invited by the police to examine the body of one of the murder victims in this case, and he was going to make the most of it. He examined the body and the bullet hole carefully. He took out a wooden pencil and poked it into the bullet hole, conferred with Doctor Watson after his own examination, then stood up and spoke to MacDonald.

'The shot that killed Mr. Snelling came from a rifle, not a pistol, and it was from far away, not close up as most might believe. The shot did not come from anyone here on the street.'

'Then where?' MacDonald asked. 'One of the buildings? If so, which one? There are so many!'

'Yes, it was one of the buildings. By using the measurements and dimensions of Mr. Snelling's body, and the speed of his walk and the length of his gait, and combining that with the trajectory of the bullet from his wound, we can discern the direction of the shooter. The shot was taken from that building over there, precisely from the eighth-floor corner office.'

MacDonald looked over and up in

surprise. 'Why, Mr. Holmes, that is the Amalgamated Insurance Building!'

'Indeed it is, and our Mr. Snelling was shot by a killer with a rifle from, I am sure, the very window where the window cleaner Barney was shot and killed not four weeks ago.'

'That canna be coincidence!' Mac-Donald blurted in anger and shock. 'I'll have my men comb that building from top to bottom!'

'No need — the assassin is already long gone, Inspector,' Holmes stated casually.

'What does that mean, Holmes?' Watson chimed in.

'It means, gentlemen, that this so-called Unseen Assassin — the man who was also known as the Boulevard Assassin of Paris years ago — is now playing his game *with* us.'

14

'Well, he has certainly earned the nickname he received from the press,' said Watson. 'No one has seen a thing, and the newspapers are going wild with this latest murder. It seems Mr. Snelling was well liked,' he continued as the two made their way back to Baker Street.

They had done all they could at the scene of the murder of Mr. Snelling. The eighth-floor room of the Amalgamated Insurance Company Building whence the shot had come had been empty. There was no evidence, and no witnesses. However, Holmes could tell that someone had been there recently.

'The window there had been opened and then closed,' he explained, 'but not all the way, and a weapon had been fired from there. The trace odor of cordite was still faintly present in the air. The few staff who work on the eighth floor were all out to lunch at the time, of course, so no one was on the floor for an entire hour. The murder was accomplished very quickly. The killer appeared to have made his escape up to the roof and then down a fire escape. As we know, no one saw anything.'

Mr. Mac shook his head in exasperation. 'The Unseen Assassin has once again done his dirty work entirely in secret.'

'Could someone who works in that building be our killer?' Watson asked briskly. It was, after all, what he supposed to be the natural question. The killer did seem to know the building and the timetable of the workers.

Holmes nodded, but without much enthusiasm. 'I suppose it is possible, but I doubt it very much. I am now sure our killer was sending us a message. He knows the Amalgamated Building quite well, not because he works there, but because he has done his research very well since he killed Barney. I believe Mr. Snelling was merely a target of opportunity — our killer was operating on a tight timetable, as the workers would be back from their lunch soon, so he had to choose someone from the crowd out on Charing Cross and kill him quickly. And he did. It was well planned. I am sure now that our killer was watching us yesterday when we visited the Amalgamated Building with Mr. Mac. So the message was sent, and received.'

'What are we to do now, Holmes?' Watson asked as the pair walked up the thirteen steps to their rooms at 221B. 'How can we even find such a man? And what kind of person does such a thing? Surely he is a monster!'

The two men entered their sitting room and made themselves comfortable. MacDonald had left them earlier and gone back to the Yard to make his report after they had made a detailed examination of the room where the shot had been fired in the insurance building. Then MacDonald told them he was going to talk to Mr. Snelling's wife and co-workers at the book shop to see what he could learn from them. Any enemies? Threats? Holmes had told MacDonald that he was sure his efforts would prove to be a waste of time, but he knew the inspector had to go through the motions of a proper investigation. They planned to meet later at Baker Street.

Holmes was silent and moody. He sat restlessly in his chair. Watson had many questions that were swirling within his mind, and it was annoying him no end that he could discern no logical answers. Holmes lit his pipe. Watson sat down in his chair and lit a cigarette. He was quiet, waiting for Holmes to speak, but not wanting to intrude upon his friend's thought process.

'I fear we have been going about this all wrong,' Holmes suddenly spoke up with a new determination in his voice. His tone sounded more confident than it had been previously, and apparently he had come to some firm decision upon the matter.

'How can that be, Holmes?' Watson asked, now even more perplexed than ever by the vagueness of this case and his companion's seeming sudden change of attitude.

'We have been looking for connections, Watson — connections that do not exist.'

'But — but you yourself said that these

murders were all connected. You told MacDonald as much, and he believes you. So do I.'

'Of course they are connected; the murders are all being done by the same man. *But it ends there,*' Holmes stated firmly. 'In fact, Watson, I believe your earlier comment about the killer, thought rather simplistic, may now have some merit.'

Watson looked at his friend curiously, some confusion showing upon his face. 'What comment?'

'I see the consternation upon your face, my friend, and believe me, I have felt that very same feeling. It is quite unsettling, but that is the truth of it. Now we shall seek to confirm or deny that theory.'

'What theory? I do not quite get what you are telling me, Holmes. Is the man some deranged maniac? Such a man may never stop his killings.'

'No, not until he is caught or killed,' Sherlock Holmes replied softly. Then the great detective went to the breakfast table and wrote out a long letter, folded it and placed it in an envelope. 'Watson, could you call down to Mrs. Hudson for her to get a boy to take this letter to the telegraph office? I need to send this message to Commandant Franco of the Surete immediately.'

'Of course, Holmes. I will see to it right away.'

15

Inspector MacDonald was at Baker Street bright and early the next morning.

'Mr. Mac, good to see you,' Holmes greeted his fellow detective in a much better mood this morning. Either a good night's sleep had done him wonders, or the new turn the case had taken in his deductions now had a positive effect upon his mind. 'We are gaining some ground. I assume there have been no further shootings overnight in London by our killer, or you would have called us.'

'You are correct; all was quiet last evening in that arena, thankfully. So what have you found out, Mr. Holmes? You have the look of the cat who has just swallowed the canary. Something is up, is it not?'

'It most certainly is, Mr. Mac. I have sent a priority telegram to Commandant Franco in Paris. He may be able to point us in a more accurate direction.'

'Aye, any direction would prove a boon at this point, Mr. Holmes. London is an enormous city, and I have no idea who our killer may be, or where to look for him. How can we catch him otherwise?'

'We shall see, Inspector,' Holmes replied with a wry knowing smile. He was now seated in his chair, long thin fingers steepled as he thought.

'Would you like a brandy while we wait, Inspector?' Watson asked, making the offer in his usual convivial manner.

'Ah, aye, that would be just the ticket now, Doctor. We hoisted a few pints the other night. Sometimes a drink or two can take the edge off. I have to tell you that this case has caused me considerable consternation at the Yard. Sir Charles Maine, my superior, is eager for a closure, and even Lestrade thinks I am barking up the wrong tree on this. He has arrested his men for the murders of Wilson and Crafts — two poor fellows are in custody even now.'

'More Hurets,' Holmes was heard to say disdainfully.

MacDonald took the glass of brandy

from Watson and downed it quickly. 'Ah, that's good stuff. Now what was that you just said, Mr. Holmes?'

'More Hurets. More innocent victims.'

'Aye, just so, I'm afraid. Dinna get me wrong — Lestrade is a good man, but he is . . . well, he is . . . '

'Unimaginative, lacking in the higher levels of competence, plodding. In short, Mr. Mac, unlike yourself, your colleague is dogged but he has no real talent.'

MacDonald smiled in acknowledgement of even a sidewise compliment, especially from the likes of a man such as Sherlock Holmes, whom he admired and respected.

'Well then, now what, Holmes?' Watson asked. He poured the inspector another round from the carved-glass decanter in his hand and poured himself one more as well.

'We wait for news from Paris.'

Inspector MacDonald nodded. 'I have nowhere to go now, and nothing to do. I spoke to the widow of Mr. Snelling, of course, and his co-workers at the bookshop. They have nothing to add to our case. There are no leads there.'

'There can be no leads in this type of case, Mr. Mac. The victims are chosen entirely at random. They are taken down serially, one after the other, like falling dominos. There is no sense to it. We were looking for motive or reason where none exists in the normal progression of things. The only logic here is that there is no logic beyond the desire to kill.'

'Sheer evil it sounds like to me,' MacDonald growled.

'It certainly says something terrible about our world that it could spawn such a devil,' Watson said, shaking his head sadly.

'Oh, I believe we shall see more and more of this in the future, my friend. As the old social orders break down, standards deteriorate and laws are not adhered to, the compulsion for less disciplined individuals to do as they will, entirely as they please — with no regard for others — will only grow. It is a sad state of affairs of our modern world.' Holmes turned away; he looked grim.

'I'll have another drink of that brandy,

Doctor, if you please,' MacDonald asked in a harsh tone.

Watson quickly poured the inspector another two fingers, and did so for himself as well. The room had taken on a rather gloomy aspect with the full import of Holmes's dire words. It was a feeling of hopelessness and impending doom, for all three men knew this killer would strike again and yet again. Would he ever be caught? What really made a man kill so thoughtlessly? Was Holmes correct that this type of murder was a harbinger of things to come? The very thought sent a chill through poor old Doctor Watson. For Watson was a man devoted to the healing arts and to life itself.

He sat down and finished his brandy. The liquor gave him a warm feeling inside as he looked carefully at Sherlock Holmes. He felt a sudden sadness for his friend now as he looked at him more closely. The man he knew as the great detective saw and understood things about the human condition that Watson knew he himself never even suspected existed. And Watson was no shrinking violet; he was a tough ex-military man and a long-time doctor who had seen his share of horror in war and upon the operating table. But this was different. He realized now the depths to which a mind like his friend's had to delve in order to achieve the miraculous solutions to some of the dark cases he took on. Poor Holmes — he was so alone, and he fought such hardened depravity; saw it face to face, day after day. How could any man stand up against it all? But Sherlock Holmes did! Oh, Holmes had his lapses, such as with the cocaine needle, and he could be surly and difficult as a partner and lodger at times; but his work was crucial. And he was successful at it. That thought suddenly turned Watson's dark imaginings more positive, for he realized that if anyone *could* get them out of this mess and find the killer, then it would be his friend, Sherlock Holmes.

'Holmes?'

'Yes, Watson?'

'You will bring this killer to book; I am sure of it. Even now he must feel the noose tightening about his neck.'

'You give me too much credit, my friend.'

'I give you not *enough* credit.'

Sherlock Holmes allowed a soft smile, sincerely touched by the praise from his long-time comrade. 'Thank you, John. You are a boon companion. Surely there is none other to match you.'

16

There was no news from Paris all that evening. MacDonald eventually left Baker Street saying he needed to go home to get some sleep. He planned to check in at the Yard the next morning, hopefully to learn there had been no more murders committed over the night. 'I will be back here tomorrow, before noon. Perhaps you will have heard some news from Paris by then, Mr. Holmes.'

'Perhaps,' Holmes replied noncommittally as MacDonald took his leave.

The waiting game progressed. Holmes was quiet. Watson felt it best not to break the silence, though he was getting an appetite, as it had been many hours since he had eaten. All he had had for sustenance since noon had been three brandies, and their temporary feeling of warmth and well-being had long since worn off.

'What do you say about taking a stroll

down to Devon's and getting a bite to eat?' Watson asked.

Holmes looked up at his friend and shrugged. 'I am not especially hungry, but it might do us good to get out of these stuffy rooms and be about for a while in the fresh night air.'

'Jolly good, Holmes! I'll get our coats and we can be off in a flash.' The doctor was happy to see his friend a bit more social and communicative, for Holmes's dark moods greatly disturbed him.

The two gentlemen went to Devon's, a rather upmarket dining establishment a few blocks away from Baker Street. The evening was cool, and a light invigorating breeze allowed them a brisk, pleasant walk. The food at Devon's proved exceptionally good, and even Holmes partook of a light evening meal. The two men enjoyed a delightful dinner without much conversation, and two hours later were on their way back to Baker Street.

Holmes and Watson walked side by side in the street, and the doctor now chatted amiably on and on about the case as Holmes seemingly listened to his words.

Watson's detective friend was trying to be polite, and the doctor knew it. It did not matter. It was a lovely evening in London and they were on their way back home after a delightful meal.

The two men came to a corner a few blocks from Baker Street when they suddenly heard the piercing report of a gunshot from behind them. Instantly the bulb of the street lamp right above Holmes exploded, raining down a hundred tiny shards of glass upon the two men.

'Get down!' Holmes shouted, pulling the doctor hard to the ground and shielding him with his own body.

'My God, Holmes! Did you see where that shot came from?' Watson barked in alarm, looking all about him in shock. He could see nothing out of the ordinary. People in the street began to run to and fro in absolute panic. A bobby whistle blew loudly.

'Just behind us. One of the buildings, one of the windows, it does not matter which one now. He is already gone.'

'But Holmes, he tried to kill you!'

'No, he is too good to miss me. He hit the target he was aiming for. He shot out the lamp above my head. That was his target. It was a warning, Watson.'

'A warning to drop the case?'

'Yes; but it will only result in making me more determined than ever to bring him down.'

'Bravo, Holmes!'

'For the beast made one major mistake: he placed *you* in danger, my friend. That is something I cannot countenance!' Holmes said in a rare display of heated anger.

Watson said not a word, but he was touched by his friend's concern for his safety. The thought that he had been in danger, also, had actually never occurred to him.

Holmes helped his friend up from the ground. 'Now, let us get back to Baker Street. Perhaps our message has arrived from Paris.'

When the two men returned to their lodgings, there was no message waiting for them. 'No telegrams, Mrs. Hudson?' Holmes asked their landlady before they walked up the steps to their sitting room.

'Sorry, Mr. Holmes. Nothing so far. No letters, no messages, no visitors, and no telegrams,' she replied with a finality that caused both men's despair to grow.

'Very well, Mrs. Hudson,' Holmes stated with obvious disappointment as he trod up the steps to 221B. 'If anything comes up . . . '

'Surely, Mr. Holmes, I will alert you immediately.'

Holmes gave her a grim little nod of his head as he slowly walked up the steps.

Once in their sitting room, Watson took up his medical bag and began to look over his friend for any wounds from the night's attack.

'I am fine, Watson.'

'I am your medical doctor, and you shall stand for an examination,' Watson insisted, and Holmes only sighed indulgently and complied.

After a quick but complete examination, the doctor proclaimed that Holmes was uninjured. He had been concerned about sharp shards of glass from the burst lamp, or a ricochet of the bullet, but thankfully Holmes was fit and uninjured.

'I told you so,' the detective chided.

'I know, but I had to check you.'

'I suppose you did, old man. Now let us get some sleep, for I have a feeling that tomorrow will be a very busy day for us.'

'All right, then good night, Holmes,' Watson said as he walked off into his bedroom on the right side of the apartment and slowly shut the door behind him.

Sherlock Holmes did not go directly into his room. Instead he sat down alone now and smoked a few pipes, his mind going over the case, eager anticipation burning within him as he awaited the news from Paris.

17

Inspector MacDonald was at Baker Street before noon the next day. He greeted Holmes and the doctor, and mentioned that there had been an event of interest that had happened the night before.

'It was near here, in fact — another shooting. Thankfully no one was hit. Apparently someone shot out a street lamp,' MacDonald stated with a shake of his head. 'A police report was made by the constable on patrol, and there was a small panic.'

'No one was arrested?' Watson asked curiously.

'No, the man made a clean getaway.'

Watson stood up. 'Well, Inspector, we know quite a bit about it. Holmes and I were there, in fact, and the shot was aimed at Holmes!'

'Not really aimed at me, Inspector, but it was our killer trying to warn me off the case,' Holmes corrected the doctor.

'I see,' MacDonald said tersely, thinking over this disturbing new development. He pulled on the ends of his long mustache. He did not like hearing of this attack, even if it was but a warning and no one was hurt. This Unseen Assassin was getting too close. Then he looked at Holmes, raising a questioning bushy eyebrow. 'I am happy that you were not injured. However, the killer could have shot you — hit you, I mean. He could have killed you. I hope you don't take this wrong, Mr. Holmes, but I wonder why he didn't do so.'

'Yes, well I cannot say for certain, Mr. Mac. It appears the shot was a warning for me to get off the case, even though I believe in some twisted manner he is actually flattered that I am involved in taking him down. He sees it as a challenge; part of his game. He may just be sending me the message that he knows I am tracking him. He is taking notice, regardless. Such is the pattern I see to his personality, and from his actions — a profile, if you will, that tells me the make-up of his particular psyche.'

'I see. Well it is good news that you were not harmed. However, you must take precautions to remain safe, Mr. Holmes.'

'That is precisely what I told him,' Watson interjected firmly.

Holmes smiled reassuringly. 'Rest assured, had the killer wanted me dead, I would even now be laying prone upon a slab in St. Bart's morgue. No, he wants me alive, so I can witness his handiwork — and I am sure he will strike again soon to show us more of his deadly work unless he is quickly stopped.'

'Aye, but we are in dire circumstances. We have no leads at all,' MacDonald growled in frustration, his thick Scottish accent breaking into his voice.

The men set down and began their wait when there was a knock on the door. Watson flew to open it, and there stood one of the loveliest sights he had ever seen before in his life. It was Mrs. Hudson, and she was holding an envelope in her hand.

'Morning, Doctor — oh, I see you have a visitor already,' she said, going on in her usual chatty manner. Holmes had already shot up from his seat, his eyes wide with excitement. 'This telegram came just now, for Mr. Holmes. It's all the way from Paris!'

'Thank you, Mrs. Hudson!' Holmes said sharply. He was already at the door and deftly snatched the envelope from his landlady's hand.

'Well, no need to be so brazen, Mr. Holmes!'

Holmes walked off with the envelope, examining it intently.

'Thank you, Mrs. Hudson,' Watson chimed in quickly with a winning smile, as he shooed her out of the room and closed the door behind her. The three men were alone now.

'Now we'll see what we shall see!' Holmes stated in an enigmatic voice while MacDonald and Watson stood beside him, looking on intently.

'Do you suppose ... ?' Watson stammered excitedly.

'I do not know for sure,' Holmes replied as he produced his letter opener and carefully sliced open the envelope and withdrew the telegram from inside. He looked at it carefully, read it fully once, nodded his head grimly, then said, 'I will read to you what Commandant Franco of the Paris Surete has to report. I posed several questions to him, and here are his replies.'

My Dear Monsieur Holmes,

Regarding your inquiry, there is one man who fits the parameters posed by your questions. That is an Englishman who was cashiered and arrested by the Legion three years ago for the murder of his captain. The man was convicted of the crime here in Paris — for the captain was a Frenchman from a high-standing family — and he was sentenced to death at the hands of madame la guillotine. However, the murderer escaped prison before justice could be meted out. This all occurred two months before Huret began his terrible Boulevard Assassinations in Paris.

This Englishman went by the name of Leslie Howarth-James. I have no further information for you other than a brief description of his physical appearance. He stands nearly six feet in height, is slim, and has short black hair. He walks with a limp, from a battle wound in his lower right leg.

I pray this information will prove to be of some assistance to you in your most worthy endeavor. At the time I did not see any indication that these two matters might be connected. I am most disturbed by these revelations. Please tell me that we did not execute the wrong man in this case.

I Remain Your Most Obedient Servant,
Jean-Francis Franco
Commandant, La Surete Nationale, Paris

'So we now see that it is not even that complicated,' Holmes remarked. 'Our killer is a man who I assumed to be a former military man — but one not in the usual terms. It is good we discovered the Paris connection to all this. That is one very real connection.'

'You mean Huret?'

'Well no, not Huret exactly. Huret was the man the French sent to the guillotine for the shootings in Paris. Not Huret, but the actual Boulevard Assassin of Paris — the man who was never caught, and got away with his crimes because of Huret. That man we now know was Leslie Howarth-James. He knew the French gendarmes had arrested the wrong man for his crimes, or he set Huret up for his crimes; so to keep things on track he stopped his murderous activities. Of course, once the murders stopped, the police were sure they had the right man. All was good in Paris. Then the man came back here — back home to England.'

'Yes, back home,' Watson said. 'So now we know that this monster who murdered people in Paris is in fact an Englishman and not French.'

'Indeed. I felt from the start that our man might be an Englishman who had been a former member of the French Foreign Legion. There are many such in the ranks; criminals and misanthropes of all kinds. The legion does not care; it takes them all. That supposition, taken with Huret and the Paris Boulevard assassinations, we now find leads to Howarth-James.'

'That works regarding your theory of the killer being a former military man, Holmes.'

'Yes, and I felt it had to be true. However, this fellow Howarth-James, London's mysterious Unseen Assassin, is a man I thought drummed out of the legion for some dire reason.'

'I would have supposed he'd just left, or retired,' Watson ventured.

'Well now we see the truth of it. The killings in Paris two years ago were much like the ones here in London now — random, brutal, full of anger and bitterness. We now know the man was forced to leave the legion for the murder of his captain — a most serious offense.'

Inspector MacDonald looked on and listened intently as Holmes and Watson discussed the case.

'Well, from what I have heard of the French Foreign Legion, they take all comers and they keep them. You have to do something pretty bad to be drummed out, and murder certainly is the worse offense,' Watson stated, for he had some idea of this by being a former military man himself.

'That is correct. Treason certainly, or the murder of a fellow legionnaire — especially an officer, and a French officer at that. Our man was, in fact, imprisoned for this crime and set for execution, but then he escaped and headed for Paris to seek his revenge.'

Watson shook his head. 'Then he is a madman.'

'No, not mad; but unrelentingly angry, viciously violent, extremely deadly, and surely evil. His anger stokes such rage that the only way he can assuage it is to resort to murder.'

'So then there is no real reason for the killing of his victims?'

'No, none whatsoever. He is doing it because in his own twisted mind, he is taking his revenge upon a world that he feels has done him wrong.'

MacDonald continued to listen with intense interest but kept silent.

Watson added, 'All right, I suppose I

am with you so far, Holmes. The man began his murder spree in Paris against the French because of his legion transgression, but he got away with his killings, and poor Huret paid the price. So he was home free, so to speak. Then why begin it all again here in London? After all, he had escaped punishment for his crimes. He had got away with it all!'

'He came home to England and tried to control his murderous rage. Look to your own medical knowledge, Watson. What does it tell you of such an aberrant personality?'

Watson thought it over carefully and nodded his agreement. 'Yes; he would be easy to anger, obsessive, obviously very violent. The more he tried *not* to slip back into his old behavior — for he is intelligent enough to realize he had got away with his crimes in Paris with poor Huret paying the price — the more he could not stop himself. He soon fell back into his old ways.'

'The power he held in his hands was just too much for him to resist,' Holmes added firmly.

'The power? You mean the power of life and death?'

'Precisely! He could not resist using that power again — and he knew he possessed it.'

'Then the man is playing God!' Watson said in outraged anger.

'Aye, doctor!' MacDonald blurted in agreement, his voice thick with anger.

'Yes, gentlemen, our killer now kills for the sheer pleasure of killing. He is playing God. He has evolved — or, more accurately, devolved. He commits his killings serially, one after another, and he derives pleasure and a sense of power from these deeds. There are no connections between him and his victims — they are mere targets of opportunity.'

There was a grim quiet that overtook the three men in that room for a long moment.

'Well, there you have it, Mr. Mac,' Holmes said in a forceful tone. 'You have your name. Now all you have to do is get your man.'

'I am amazed by the truth of it all now. And did you note, Mr. Holmes, that our culprit possesses a rather prestigious name? By my reckoning, this Leslie Howarth-James fellow may be one of the sons of the Earl of Westron, if I am not mistaken.'

'You are not mistaken,' Sherlock Holmes spoke up. 'In fact, he is the third son of the earl. A son who will never inherit, so he chose to make his mark in the military, like so many of the second and third sons of the nobility must do these days.'

'I see,' MacDonald replied, nodding his head.

'But really, of all things, the legion of France!' Watson interjected curiously, some annoyance creeping into his tone. 'Why not our own fine British army, as most all later sons of the nobility do?'

'Yes, why not? We shall find that out soon enough,' Holmes stated with a nod of his head. 'Quickly, now — we must take action right away on this news!'

18

'Then I must be off immediately and make the arrest,' MacDonald said. 'I will have every member of the Yard and the Metropolitan Police out looking for this man. I shall go immediately to his family home and speak with the earl.' He quickly picked up his coat and hat; but before he rushed out, he added, 'By any chance, would you two gentlemen like to accompany me?'

'Surely! I mean — we would be most honored,' Watson replied in a hearty tone.

Sherlock Holmes merely nodded his approval, then added, 'This Unseen Assassin will not remain unseen for too long now, I think. We must get to him quickly.'

The ride out to Kent was rapid but invigorating. Kent is known as the garden of England, and it is a lush land of greenery and colorful flowers that make it a most convivial landscape. Holmes,

Watson and MacDonald, along with three constables the inspector had picked up from the nearest town, spoke about the case as their carriage ate up the miles to the estate of the earl.

'We know this third son, Leslie, left England to join the French Foreign Legion,' MacDonald stated curiously. 'But I wonder why.'

'I would venture that being the third son of an earl, he would never stand to inherit the estate or the titles, so he would have to make his own way in the world as so many other later siblings of the nobility are forced to do,' Watson offered, looking at Holmes, who nodded approvingly.

'Go on, Watson; you are doing fine,' Holmes encouraged.

'Well, then, the legion is known as a repository for men from all over the world, and from all classes. Men who seek adventure or yearn for action — many being former military men who crave the excitement of battle once again. They come from every country in the world, but take an oath to fight under the French flag and for France, and they serve under French officers.'

'Quite right, Watson,' Holmes continued as the carriage cut a quick swath over the country dirt road to the earl's home. 'However, you left out the most important aspect of the true allure of the legion. It is a place where a man can go to become lost. Now our romantic writers such as Mr. Wren tell rousing stories of men who have lost in love, or have become so distraught in life that they seek solace in the ranks of the legion, and to have their names placed in the rolls of honor — and I suppose that may be true in some cases. They seek to forget. However, far more realistic is the fact that criminals of all kinds — thieves, murderers, rapists, and worse; take your pick — run off to join the legion to escape their punishment and to live out their lives free from prison. For what a man was, or what he did before he joined the legion, means nothing anymore once he has joined the ranks.'

'I see,' Watson said.

'Aye, but do you think our young Leslie may have had some other reason to escape to the legion?' MacDonald asked carefully as the carriage quickly rambled over the rough country road.

'Yes, I believe so. He is a man who by his actions has shown us he is extremely violent and volatile. We can tell that by what we see in the patterns of his behavior, or in his personal profile. Such a man cannot evade his true nature and his natural tendencies for long — and there must be some record of it from even back in his youth. There will be some trace of it there, I am sure. Some warning sign of the monster that is to come, when he grows older,' Holmes stated confidently.

The carriage rode on. They had already traveled two hours and were approaching their destination.

'I have informed the Yard and the Metropolitan Police,' MacDonald said. 'Men are out now scouring all parts of London, looking for a man of Howarth-James's description with a right-leg limp from a war wound. The boys have instructions from on high to collect all likely suspects and bring them in. We shall see what they come up with later, Mr. Holmes.'

'But while your men are certainly thorough and may be sure to catch the usual criminal in their dragnet, I rather think not with this fellow. We are pursuing a wily adversary, one whose penchant for escape is only eclipsed by his violent actions. A most dangerous antagonist,' Holmes added.

'The Unseen Assassin,' Watson said thoughtfully. 'The press were correct about him — he has remained unseen and un-detected.'

'Until now, Watson! Until now! Soon we shall have him. We are closing in; and as you have said, the noose is closing in on him too,' Holmes replied with firm determination.

19

The estate of Sir Alfred Howarth-James, Earl of Westron, was grand and enormous. The pathway to the main house — a palace, actually — went on for over a mile through some of the most beautiful greenery and colorful flower gardens the men had ever seen in the English countryside.

'Truly this is a glorious garden out here, Mr. Holmes,' MacDonald said.

Sherlock Holmes did not reply. He was busy thinking, turning over the facts of the case in his mind. All ancillary items, like graceful trees and well-manicured greenery, and the riotous colors of so many bright flowers and gardens, as lovely as they might be, did not intrude upon his thoughts at all. Watson, however, was captivated by the landscape and the breathtaking beauty of the place.

'That such a lovely place could spawn such a terrible monster,' the doctor whispered under his breath. MacDonald just shook his head in agreement.

They reached the house soon enough, and the trio quickly got out of the carriage. 'Remain here; I will call you if I need you,' MacDonald ordered the three constables who had accompanied them in the carriage. Then the trio approached the door of the mansion, which suddenly opened before MacDonald could knock. A livered butler, looking more like a military officer, stood tall and firm in the doorway.

'Gentlemen, you are expected,' was all the man said by way of greeting. 'Will you please follow me?'

Watson looked at Holmes and Mac-Donald curiously. 'We are expected?'

Holmes nodded. 'Apparently.'

'Well I for one never communicated with the earl or any of his staff,' MacDonald added. 'I never said a word. I thought it best that we come out here quickly and that it be a surprise visit.'

'Well, it does not appear to be a surprise at all,' Holmes stated dryly.

'No, it does not,' MacDonald grumbled in anger. Someone in London had surely let the cat out of the bag, either by accident or intentionally. In any case, it was bad news.

The trio followed the butler into the house and down a long foyer. The mansion was exquisite. MacDonald had seen nothing like it in his life before. Perhaps Lady Westcott's mansion in London came the closest — he had been inside it on that case years ago. The home of John Douglas in Brilstone, from the earlier case that Watson had written about under the title 'The Valley of Fear', had also been fine. However, the earl's home and estate were altogether something different. This was a place that shouted of wealth and great power.

'Good lord, it's like Buckingham Palace in here!' MacDonald blurted in rapt awe. The building certainly was huge, made of bright white marble and exquisite rare woods, and everywhere were statues, paintings, priceless furniture, rare vases; an array of riches. Renaissance tapestries gilded in gold hung from the walls.

'Have you ever been inside Buckingham Palace?' Watson asked the inspector.

'No, but I have passed by it many times, and this looks like I imagine it would inside.'

'Come now, gentlemen, do not dawdle,' the butler prodded the three men rather impatiently. 'His lordship is awaiting your arrival.'

'How did the earl know we were coming?' MacDonald asked the butler, annoyed that word of his visit here had somehow got out before he had even arrived.

The butler stopped, turned and looked fully into the face of Inspector Mac-Donald, his face betraying nothing. 'I am not at liberty to discuss that, sir. Perhaps the earl himself will divulge that information when you see him. He is most anxious to speak with you. I can tell you this: the earl is a man with many friends in high places, so there is very little that happens of which he is not aware.'

'Yes, of course,' Holmes said. 'Lead on, if you please.'

The butler bowed, and continued to lead the trio to a large and sumptuously appointed library. The room was very spacious, being surrounded by floor-to-ceiling bookshelves set against all four walls. The shelves were stuffed with fine leather bindings. There must have been a fortune in rare books upon them.

There was a man standing in the center of the room, apparently awaiting the trio. He was old but stood ramrod stiff, having a military posture and fiery eyes that belied his advanced years. There was a younger man beside him, and both were dressed in modest attire, almost as if huntsmen or gamekeepers, rather than the noble lords who were the inhabitants of this luxurious mansion.

The butler spoke in a firm tone, 'Gentlemen, I have the honor of presenting his lordship Sir Alfred Howarth-James, Earl of Westron, and his first son and heir, Jeremy Howarth-James. My lord, this is Scotland Yard Inspector Alec MacDonald, Mr. Sherlock Holmes, and Doctor John Watson, come down from London to see you.'

'Thank you, Reggie. You may leave us now,' the earl said as he and his son came to welcome and shake hands with the trio of visitors. They seemed affable enough, and possessed a more common touch that made the trio of visitors feel comfortable and welcome in their presence.

'Yes, my lord,' the butler replied and quickly left the room, silently closing the door behind him.

'Well, Inspector — or should I say, Mr. Holmes? Yes, I am aware of your activities, and applaud them! You are here on some business, I am told, regarding my son Leslie?'

'Your lordship,' Holmes replied in a level tone, 'do you know where Leslie may be? We need to know his whereabouts, or where he is living now. I assume he does not reside here?'

'No, Mr. Holmes, Inspector. You see, my son and I have been estranged for many years. Irrevocably estranged. He is a blight upon this house and my good name, and I disown him entirely! I have no knowledge of his whereabouts at all.'

'My father has not seen my brother in almost ten years,' Jeremy added by way of explanation.

'I see,' Holmes said as he looked at the

earl's son closely.

'They had a falling out. There has been no contact, nor would my father initiate or accept any contact from Leslie.'

The earl growled out in evident disdain, 'He is out of the will and shall never inherit, gentlemen. When I shuffle off this mortal coil, my first son, Jeremy here, will become earl and retain the estate, properties and titles. My second son, Tyrone, will also be well looked after. But my third son, the black sheep, Leslie, shall receive nothing. He is a vile misanthrope, a despicable person lacking in any honor — he dishonors my very name. I admit that it hurts me deeply to say this, but the stark truth of it, gentlemen, is that my third son is just no damn good!'

There was an uncomfortable muted silence for a long moment at that sharp statement.

'Can you tell me, your lordship,' Holmes began carefully, 'the reason for the rift between you and your son, Leslie? And the final event that severed your ties to him permanently?'

The earl looked uncomfortable. It was obviously a topic that he found most distasteful to discuss.

'Father, please. Innocent people have been killed.'

The earl nodded his head. 'Yes, of course. I have always done my duty, gentlemen, and I shall do so now, no matter how distasteful. Leslie was always . . . different. Even as a young lad, he had violent tendencies. I have no idea how he obtained this aspect of his personality, or where it originated. He was forever in trouble as a child, and he grew to become the most accomplished liar and scoundrel I have ever come across. And that is saying a lot, let me tell you, gentlemen! Well, as you can believe, it caused me great pain. I also discovered that as a boy he bullied and terrorized the servants and staff. It ran far beyond mere entitlement of the wealthy, or simply being spoiled — for he was not spoiled; but I caught him in the middle of deplorable actions many times. It disturbed me greatly. Why, Leslie even intimidated and compelled the staff to hand over to him part of their salaries, even their birthday and Christmas bonus money!'

Jeremy explained proudly, 'My father has always been a most generous master to our servants and staff.' You could clearly see the admiration evident there of the son for the father. 'Our people are all loyal and have been with us for many years, in some cases generations. Our butler, Reggie, whom you have met, has been with my family for more than 30 years.'

'I see,' Holmes allowed with a knowing nod of his head. 'So young Leslie is a bad penny.'

'A bad penny, sir!' exclaimed the earl. 'That hardly says it at all. He is the very devil himself, Mr. Holmes! And I say that in great sadness, but with full knowledge that you know I am his father.'

'Please go on,' Holmes requested in a calm tone, though he was most interested now.

The earl shook his head and pursed his lips as if to get a bad taste out of his mouth. 'That man you met, Reggie — he had a daughter once. A lovely young daughter. My son Leslie took . . . well, he took advantage of her most terribly. I cannot even speak of it!'

The son continued, 'Mr. Holmes, Leslie raped the poor girl, and she died because of the violence of my brother's attack. Leslie said it was an accident, but it did not seem to be so from the evidence at the time. We — my father and I, and Reggie — believe it was cold-blooded murder. At the time, Leslie was arrested for the crime, but he never saw trial. He effected an escape, and we lost track of him after that.'

'And good riddance!' the earl grunted. 'Poor Reggie. What my son did to that man's poor girl . . . '

'And this Reggie has remained with you since then?' MacDonald asked, showing some disbelief at the story.

'Yes; Reggie is a most loyal servant, actually more of a friend and companion to my father,' Jeremy added by way of explanation. 'They comforted each other; for you see, Reggie lost a daughter and my father lost a son. Reggie took solace in his work — a most loyal retainer — and no more was ever spoken of Leslie or the deed done to Reggie's poor daughter in this house since then.'

'I have not seen or heard from Leslie since then, Mr. Holmes,' the earl added, 'and I hope that I never do. He is dead to me. Had I but only known his true nature, I would have strangled the life out of him as he lay in his crib as an infant!' The old earl was now in tears. Hiding them with his hands as he walked off, and turning his back, he left the room, which remained quiet for a long moment afterward.

'You have to forgive my father, gentlemen; he has been through much turmoil with Leslie, and it has been a heavy burden for him — and us all,' Jeremy stated casually. 'Now, is there anything else I can do for you before you leave? Your presence here is upsetting the household. Poor Reggie need not be reminded of the events of years ago.'

'I understand,' Holmes said as the earl's son led the trio out of the library and into the spacious open hall.

'Reggie, these gentlemen are leaving

now. Will you kindly show them to their carriage.'

'Yes, sir. Gentlemen, please follow me.'

20

As Watson and the inspector trailed behind the butler, they looked back at Holmes, who was still standing at the other end of the hall with the earl's son, Jeremy.

'Go on; I will be with you in a moment,' Holmes told his companions in a tone that brooked no refusal.

The butler led MacDonald and Watson to the front door of the massive home. They were soon led around a corner and out of the view of Holmes and Jeremy.

'A very sad story,' Holmes said to the earl's son. 'I have learned that your brother escaped England and fled to Paris, where he joined the French Foreign Legion to lose himself.'

'So I have heard now from the inspector,' Jeremy replied.

'Well, I have just one more question to ask you, if you please.'

'Of course. What is it?'

'Your father told us he has not seen your brother since his escape from England, and I believe him. But you have never stated this yourself. Why is that, I wonder? I think I know. If you would be so kind, I need you to give me the address where you send the money to your brother. He needs it to live on and would have rather expensive tastes, I am sure.'

'Whatever do you mean? What are you saying?'

'Oh come now. Your father may not know where your brother Leslie is living, but you certainly do, and I know that you send him money. I even believe you effected his original escape from England, but I will not go into that now. So be truthful with me, and this need never get out. I am not the official police; I just want the truth so we can stop the killings. You must cooperate — your brother is a monster, as you are well aware!' Holmes stated forcefully, and the full power of his voice cowed the young noble.

'You would tell my father?' Jeremy said nervously. Obviously he was fearful of hurting the old lion, whom he greatly respected and admired.

'Yes, I would tell him — all of it — and the police if need be,' Holmes replied, and his tone brooked no denial.

The earl's son thought that over very quickly and realized he had no choice in the matter. 'I hope that if I am truthful with you, I may trust you, Mr. Holmes.'

'I am the very soul of discretion in these sensitive matters.'

'Very well. What my father told you was all true. Leslie evaded the murder charge and arrest. And you are correct — I helped him escape. I thought if he had a second chance in a new country away from England, he might change his ways. He was my brother, after all, Mr. Holmes — a bad sort to be sure, but I could not stand by while he had no chance in life because of one terrible mistake. I see now that this was all because of me. It seems I have much to be judged for.'

'You need to work that out yourself and with God. What I need now is the truth.'

Jeremy nodded. 'We had not heard from my brother in years. Then one day a few months ago, I chanced to meet him in central London. I was on the way to the bank when I found myself accosted by a disreputable man with overgrown hair and a beard, in ragged clothing, and was shocked when I recognized that it was my long-lost brother Leslie. He was newly returned from Paris, he told me, and was in desperate need of funds and a place to live.

'Well, I was shocked by his sudden appearance, but overjoyed to see him again after so many years. Time had healed some of our differences, but still I was hesitant, as Leslie had always been so volatile. My anger with him was not as deep as my father's, but I did know that my brother was a bad weed that needed to be plucked out of the garden. He proved it soon enough by using our family ties to demand money.

'Of course I was willing to help, so I gave him what I had on me at the time — ten pounds; but he just laughed. I was shocked by his behavior and demeanor. He took the money I gave him, then demanded five hundred pounds more! He told me that if I did not pay up, he would go to Father and tell him I had helped him to escape. It would have devastated him, and placed me in an uncomfortable position with the law. I could not let that happen. By the look of my brother, I could see he had fallen on hard times, and perhaps fate had dealt him a more cruel hand in life than justice and the courts ever could have done. He looked terrible, so I took pity on him and decided to help him.'

'You gave him more money.'

'Only enough to live decently, to buy food and put a roof over his head. I know he has a one-room loft in Whitechapel; quite a rough spot in the old town. I bring him food and some cash there — a hundred pounds or so, every month. That is all I have to do with him, Mr. Holmes. I know nothing of what he does or how he lives. We speak little. I do the absolute least I can for him out of former brotherly love. He is my brother, after all. Can you not understand?'

'I have a brother as well,' Holmes said softly, thinking of Mycroft and their tangled relationship, 'though our situation is nothing like your own.'

'I am sure it is not. Nothing can be like it is with Leslie.'

'I see. But you also helped him out of fear that he would go to your father and the police.'

'Yes, of course. It would kill my father after all these years to see Leslie again. Regarding the police — I do not care, knowing what I know now. My brother has done terrible things, Mr. Holmes. He tormented me and our other siblings as children. We were all glad to be rid of him. However, I had no idea he was responsible for these killings recently reported in London. Of that I shall forever be ashamed.'

'How many months has Leslie been blackmailing you?'

'What? Blackmail, you say?'

'Of course; were you not aware of it? His threat to go to your father and the police, his demands for money — it is plainly blackmail, pure and simple, though obviously couched in delicate brotherly terms of dire need.'

The earl's first son looked glum; he had

never thought of it in those precise words before. He was obviously not the type of man to think that way of people, especially his own brother, and it quite unnerved him. 'Blackmail! My God, I had no idea.'

'I believe you did not know,' Holmes stated firmly. 'Now, can you give me that address in Whitechapel?'

'Yes, of course. I am sorry, Mr. Holmes; truly my father and I had no idea what Leslie was up to until this morning, just before your arrival. One of my father's friends at Scotland Yard — you know he has connections in high places — told us that the police now believe Leslie was responsible for the 'Unseen Assassin' murders reported by the press in London. I must admit that it never occurred to me that it could be my very own brother Leslie doing such terrible things — but now that I know about it, I am not surprised. Nor is my poor father. He is loath to discuss the matter, as am I; for it is a grave matter of family shame, and a stain upon the family honor.'

'No stain upon you or your father,' Holmes offered politely, putting a reassuring hand on the young man's shoulder in a kindly gesture. 'These kinds of things hit a family hard, and often for no apparent reason, for evil seeks its own actions for its own ends. Now, give me that address in Whitechapel, and my companions and I will be off and you need never see us again.'

Jeremy took out a notepad and pencil, then quickly wrote down a street name and building number and handed the paper to Holmes. 'He is still my brother, and I still love him as a brother, Mr. Holmes. That is why I helped him against my father's wishes. But please make sure the police stop him. He cannot be allowed to continue these killings — and if it means he himself must be killed, then so be it. I would even welcome it.'

21

Upon their return to London, Inspector MacDonald immediately assembled a flying squad and with Holmes and Watson, went directly to the address Holmes had been given in Whitechapel by Jeremy.

The area was dark, even in the daylight. It was a dank, morbid part of the city full of filthy hovels and tenement dwellings for the poor and the destitute. No hope resided in these streets. There were no numbers on the buildings, but MacDonald and his men found the one they were seeking easily enough.

'The loft upstairs is where his room is located,' Holmes said softly.

'True, but my men will take the entire building,' MacDonald stated as he pointed to some of the members of his special flying squad. 'You men will come inside with Mr. Holmes, the Doctor and myself. You others will stand guard out here in the front — while you men go secure the back exit. No one gets away, do you understand? Use your firearms if you must!'

The flying squad men, unlike the usual London bobbies or Scotland Yard detectives, comprised a special branch who were allowed to carry firearms and were well versed in their use.

'All right, are you ready?' MacDonald asked. His men nodded eagerly.

Watson looked over at Holmes, whose face was simply impassive. He wondered what thoughts were going on in his friend's mind, now that they were so close to finally catching the Unseen Assassin of London.

'Good, then go ahead! Knock it down and go in!' MacDonald ordered his men, and the flying squad burst open the door and ran into the building, guns drawn, fanning out into every room, and then moving up the shaky steps to the loft and one room up there that was their destination. The movement was fast and furious; the men were in and had the entire building immediately under their control. They met with no resistance

— for the building was empty!

'He's not here! Flown the crib! Maybe even London!' MacDonald blurted, totally put off by the results of his tightly planned actions. He had been told by a fellow out on the street that the man they were looking for — the slim man with the limp — would be here inside the building, but he was not. They had apparently just missed him.

Holmes examined the room in the loft. It was a stinking hovel. No man other than an opium addict would choose to live in such a place. Holmes knew that, being given a hundred pounds a month from his brother, Leslie had to have another place, and a better, in which to live. He looked over the room carefully, then nodded.

'Sorry, Holmes,' Watson said, sharing the disappointment of his friend.

'It is just a drop, but that does not mean . . . ' Holmes said thoughtfully; then he grew silent.

'What is it, Holmes? You seem to have come to some decision,' Watson asked his friend.

'Yes; a man who is being given a

hundred pounds each month by his brother to live would not choose to stay in a hovel such as this. This is the drop, or a layabout — a hideout; not his true residence.'

'Then we need to find where he is living. But how do we do that?' Watson asked, allowing his utter frustration to show through. He had been so hopeful that they would catch the monster now, that missing him was a cruel blow.

'Hello, what have we here?' Sherlock Holmes was at one of the windows, looking down into the crowd that had gathered in the street below them. Nothing unusual about that; crowds always gathered during police action and raids, especially in these poorer sections of the city. With a keen eye, Holmes scanned the many men who made up the crowd, suddenly shouting down to the constables MacDonald had stationed in the street at the front of the building. Pointing out a man in the crowd, Holmes shouted, 'Stop that man! The man in the black cap with the limp — stop him!'

The men of the flying squad looked up

at Holmes, and then at the man he had pointed to in the crowd, who had just run off down the street with a noticeable limp in his right leg that slowed him down a bit.

'Stop him! Stop that man with the black cap and the limp!' MacDonald now also commanded his men, who were now off like wild dogs on the chase.

22

'Well, Mr. Holmes, my men caught him. Mr. Leslie Howarth-James, the Unseen Assassin of London, finally brought to book, thanks to you,' Inspector MacDonald told his consulting detective friend with a deep sigh of relief. He was now once again at Baker Street, giving Holmes and Doctor Watson his update on the case. 'My boys are dogged fellows,' he continued. 'They brought him down a few streets away from his Whitechapel hovel. Now he has a new address, in a cell in Scotland Yard,' the inspector added with pride.

'Bravo!' Watson could no longer restrain his joy, for the entire affair had been most unnerving and convoluted. Why, the killer had even taken a shot at Holmes himself! Even though it had only been a warning, it had still placed his friend in danger.

'What will be done with him, Mr. Mac?' Holmes asked the inspector.

'Well, it has all become rather political

now, Mr. Holmes, as you might guess. Our man, who was responsible for the murders here in London, also committed the earlier murders in Paris. The French have put in a prior claim for him, and he will get the death penalty there — the guillotine, so I believe the decision will come from the Home Office that he is to be sent back to France for justice.'

'That seems fair,' Watson stated.

'Yes, I agree,' Holmes replied. 'A death penalty here by hanging, or one by madame la guillotine in Paris, is of no consequence so long as Leslie Howarth-James pays the ultimate price for his many crimes.'

'Justice is served!' Watson spoke up with gusto.

'Yes, and the case of the Unseen Assassin is closed — thank God!' Inspector MacDonald replied in a stern voice. Then in a much softer tone he said, 'Well, gentlemen — Mr. Holmes — I want to thank you both for all your help.'

'It is nothing, Mr. Mac,' Holmes replied with a slight grin. 'Watson and I were more than happy to assist you in this case and help bring it to a close.'

'You certainly made the difference, I will admit that. If not for you both, that man would still be out there in London killing our innocent citizens.'

'I shudder at the very thought!' Watson added with a slight shiver.

'I am well satisfied with the result, Mr. Mac,' Holmes stated with an imperceptible nod of his head.

'What now, MacDonald?' Watson asked curiously.

'Well, I leave for Paris in two days' time, with an escort, to bring the prisoner back for French justice. I will deliver him to the French authorities in Paris, and they shall carry out their duty.'

'Then a safe journey to you, Mr. Mac, and do come and visit us upon your return and fill in for us the final details if you please.'

'Of course, Mr. Holmes.'

'Then, as the French say, Watson and I bid you *adieu*.'

23

One week later, Mrs. Hudson knocked soundly upon the door of 221B, announcing there was a visitor, and Watson let Scotland Yard Inspector Alec MacDonald into their sitting room.

'Ah, Mr. Mac, back already and newly returned from Paris I see,' Holmes said as he came over and shook the hand of the man he considered to be the most talented on the London police force.

'Aye, Mr. Holmes. As I promised, I have returned to report to you about the final disposition of this case, and to deliver to you something.'

'Really? I have no idea what that could be, but pray tell us what happened with Howarth-James,' Holmes asked eagerly.

'Yes, so you returned him to the French authorities. Did all go along smoothly? I hope the man did not try any escape,' Watson said curiously; for who knew what the sinister monster was capable of?

'No, no worries there, Doctor. The delivery went off without a hitch and the French authorities took all well in hand. The blade was dropped, the execution was performed, and the villain's head was quite neatly separated from his shoulders. I viewed the execution personally, and I can tell you that the man who seemed the least affected by the entire incident was the man who was executed. He showed no emotion at all. Most strange, isn't it, Mr. Holmes?'

'The ways of criminals are often incomprehensible to law-abiding folk.'

'But not to you.'

'No, not to me.'

'Well, he probably had given up and accepted his fate,' Watson chimed in.

'I do not think so,' Holmes added thoughtfully.

'Well, whatever the reason, the man is dead and the case is closed,' MacDonald said, breaking out with a wide grin of victory.

'Thank God!' Watson added with evident relief.

'Now, Mr. Holmes,' MacDonald continued, 'I have this small package to deliver to you from Commandant Franco of the French Surete. Upon my arrival in Paris with the prisoner, he questioned me in detail upon all aspects of the case. He was most avidly interested, and of course I told him of your part in it all. He told me to tell you that he was very grateful for your assistance; and the next day before I left for home, he gave me this package with the instructions that I was to deliver it to you personally.'

'Whatever is it?' Watson asked. It was a rather small package.

'I have no idea. Franco would not tell me. Here, Mr. Holmes, you open it. It is addressed to you,' MacDonald said with a smile and a twist of his large mustache. He handed the package over carefully. It was obvious that he knew it was of some importance. Holmes took the proffered package and looked it over closely.

'Open it!' Watson blurted in excitement.

Holmes smiled indulgently, took out his pen knife and cut the paper wrapping. Inside were two letters and a smaller package.

'Here, Watson, will you do the honors,

please?' Holmes asked, handing the package to the doctor.

'Of course.' Watson took the package, unfolded the first letter, and began reading out loud.

Monsieur Sherlock Holmes,

Greetings. I write to officially thank you for your assistance in this serious criminal matter that has plagued my country for some years now. I have passed on news about your contribution in this affair to our President, Monsieur Carnot, and he has expressed his wish to write to you personally. His letter is enclosed forthwith.

Once Again I Remain Your Obedient Servant,
Franco, Commandant, La Surete Nationale, Paris.

'Quite amazing, Mr. Holmes!' MacDonald stated. 'Now read the other letter, Doctor.'

'Here it is,' Watson said with some awe. 'It is from the president of the French Republic!'

Monsieur Sherlock Holmes,

My dear sir, I wish to express to you the sincere appreciation of the French people and myself for your valued assistance in this most heinous criminal matter and your good work in ensuring that the true criminal was brought to French justice. The fact that an innocent man was originally executed for these crimes will forever be a stain upon France, but your efforts have brought the true latter to justice. For that, I and all of France are most grateful.

In honor of your contribution to the people of France and the French Republic, it is my pleasure to present you with this token of our great esteem and affection. It is the Ordre National de la Legion d'Honneur. Wear it well, Mr. Sherlock Holmes. God Bless you, sir, and vive la France!

I Am And Remain Your Most Obedient Servant,
Marie Francois Sadi Carnot,
Fifth President of the Third French Republic.

'What is it, Doctor?' MacDonald asked eagerly.

Watson fumbled with the small object that had been enclosed with the letters. It was an ornate red velvet pouch with a silver drawstring at the end. The doctor deftly opened the pouch and withdrew from it what proved to be an exquisite green and white ten-pointed medal that hung below a green wreath and a red ribbon. The beauty of the item fairly took Watson's breath away.

Sherlock Holmes looked on intently but remained silent.

'I believe — no, I am certain!' Watson stammered in awe. 'Holmes, there is no mistake — you have been given the Order of The Legion of Honor! Here it is, given by the French president himself! Why, it is exquisite!'

Sherlock Holmes slowly nodded, accepting the bauble when Watson handed it over to him. He examined it carefully, then silently read the president's letter himself. He smiled slowly. 'Ah, those French. So emotional — so *French*.' Then, as if they were mere everyday items in his usual detective work, Holmes took the two letters and the medal and placed them in the top drawer of his desk. He shut the drawer and walked away, a slight smile playing across his thin lips.

'Well congratulations, Holmes!' Watson shouted in unrestrained joy for his friend's good fortune. 'This is a great honor, and well deserved!'

'Yes, Mr. Holmes; I wish to offer you my congratulations also,' said MacDonald. 'Very well done! You know, we are all proud of you at the Yard. Even Lestrade the other day was saying to me, 'Where would we be without our Mr. Sherlock Holmes?''

'Lestrade said that, did he?' Holmes asked dubiously.

'Yes,' MacDonald said with a slight grin. 'Or words to that effect.'

'Mr. Mac, I do believe you are fudging. At least Lestrade has released the poor men he has arrested for the Unseen Assassin killings — there will be no more Hurets on my watch!'

'Yes, Mr. Holmes, he has released the men,' MacDonald replied firmly.

'Well, Holmes, all in all, a good bit of work. I am so very proud of you,' Watson spoke up, unable to hide the admiration he felt for this most special of men.

'Oh poppycock, old man. I am merely a consulting detective. I consult on crimes to bring the perpetrators to justice; that is all. It is who I am and what I do, and I will do it until the end of my days — eh, Watson?'

'Of course, Holmes. And I will be with you, at your side, until the end of my days as well.'

'Then — the niceties of presidential letters and gaudy medals notwithstanding — I could not ask for a more pleasant journey through this life than that.'

Historical Note

The case of Huret, The Boulevard Assassin, was originally only a brief mention in the Sherlock Holmes story 'The Adventure of the Golden Pince-Nez' by Doyle, which was originally published in 1904 in *The Strand* magazine. However, there is a ten-year span between the time the case actually occurred in 1894 and when Watson mentioned it later in 'Pince-Nez' in 1904. The delay in the telling of this case was perhaps due to the unstable political upheavals in the French Republic at the time.

In 'Pince-Nez', Watson tells us the case was set in 1894 and adds, ' . . . the tracking and arrest of Huret, the Boulevard Assassin — an exploit which won for Holmes an autograph letter of thanks from the French president and the Order of The Legion of Honor.' In fact, we have now discovered that there was quite a bit more to this story than good old Watson at first let on. Not at all that unusual.

France in the early 1890s was a land in violent turmoil; die-hard revolutionaries and socialist anarchists were committing many terrorist acts, including assassinations of government officials and bombings in public places. The country was in chaos and the government was under severe pressures. Various anarchist terrorists had been arrested for these crimes, and two executions of major criminal anarchists occurred before the summer of 1894. The situation had by then reached a dangerous point in the nation's history, and the future of France seemed to hang in the balance.

The anarchist assault on France would continue, marking 1894 a dark and deadly year in French history. On June 25 of that year, Marie Francois Sadi Carnot, Fifth President of the Third Republic, was assassinated — stabbed to death by an Italian anarchist. The nation was thrown into turmoil and deep mourning. This was bare weeks after his letter and the award of the medal to Holmes.

Later that year, there would be another severe blow to the glory of France. That was when the notorious Dreyfus Case began, where an innocent French army officer was convicted of treason and imprisoned on Devil's Island. Dreyfus was convicted because he was a Jew, which highlighted the severe strain of anti-Semitism that ran through the French nation, and which would remain until the fall of France against Germany in World War II and the rise of the Vichy regime that collaborated with the Nazis. Meanwhile, anarchists throughout Europe continued to spread terror and murder across the continent after the assassination of the French president in 1894.

Even the United States was not immune, for in 1901 President William McKinley was assassinated by a man who, after hearing a speech by anarchist and future communist Emma Goldman, wanted to do something for the anarchist cause. Twenty years after the Unseen Assassin case, in August 1914, one more anarchist would assassinate Archduke Ferdinand of the Austro-Hungarian Empire, which would precipitate the horrors of World War I.

While the name of Huret is not listed today in any of the French history texts, it is possible he was one of the many players who participated in some minor way in these terrorist acts. The random killings of Parisians — blamed on him — contributed to the destabilization of French society, which is what the anarchists were seeking to achieve. In any case, Watson and Holmes's involvement in the case shows that it was much more convoluted than the good doctor only originally hinted at in 'Pince-Nez'. In fact, while we now know that Huret was an innocent man, albeit a rabble-rouser and anarchist himself, the true killer along the Paris boulevards was Leslie Howarth-James.

Howarth-James was not an anarchist at all, but an early manifestation of what is today called a serial killer. Holmes also used a new manner of detection in this case that would become known as the practice of criminal profiling. Holmes, as always, was ahead of the curve when it came to solving crime.

We know Watson sometimes played loose with the facts in the information he included in his Holmes stories — sometimes out of error, sometimes due to a lapse in memory; but more often it was in order to hide the true names of certain major participants in a case to protect their identity. There is no mention of any Earl of Westron in the books of British nobility, and there is no Howarth-James family existing at the time this story takes place either, so it is difficult to determine just which noble British family — though obviously possessing great wealth and power — Watson was writing about, or seeking to give cover to. Perhaps we will never know.

The Order of the Legion of Honor is the highest medal given for military and civil merits presented by the French government. It was established by Napoleon Bonaparte in 1802. There are five degrees of distinction of The Order, with the highest being a *chevalier*, or knight, which was the honor given to Sherlock Holmes in 1894. In the author's opinion, no one deserved it more!

We do hope that you have enjoyed reading this large print book.

Did you know that all of our titles are available for purchase?

We publish a wide range of high quality large print books including:
Romances, Mysteries, Classics
General Fiction
Non Fiction and Westerns

Special interest titles available in large print are:
The Little Oxford Dictionary
Music Book, Song Book
Hymn Book, Service Book

Also available from us courtesy of Oxford University Press:
Young Readers' Dictionary
(large print edition)
Young Readers' Thesaurus
(large print edition)

For further information or a free brochure, please contact us at:
Ulverscroft Large Print Books Ltd.,
The Green, Bradgate Road, Anstey,
Leicester, LE7 7FU, England.
Tel: (00 44) **0116 236 4325**
Fax: (00 44) **0116 234 0205**